ANTIQUE
FAIRY
TALES

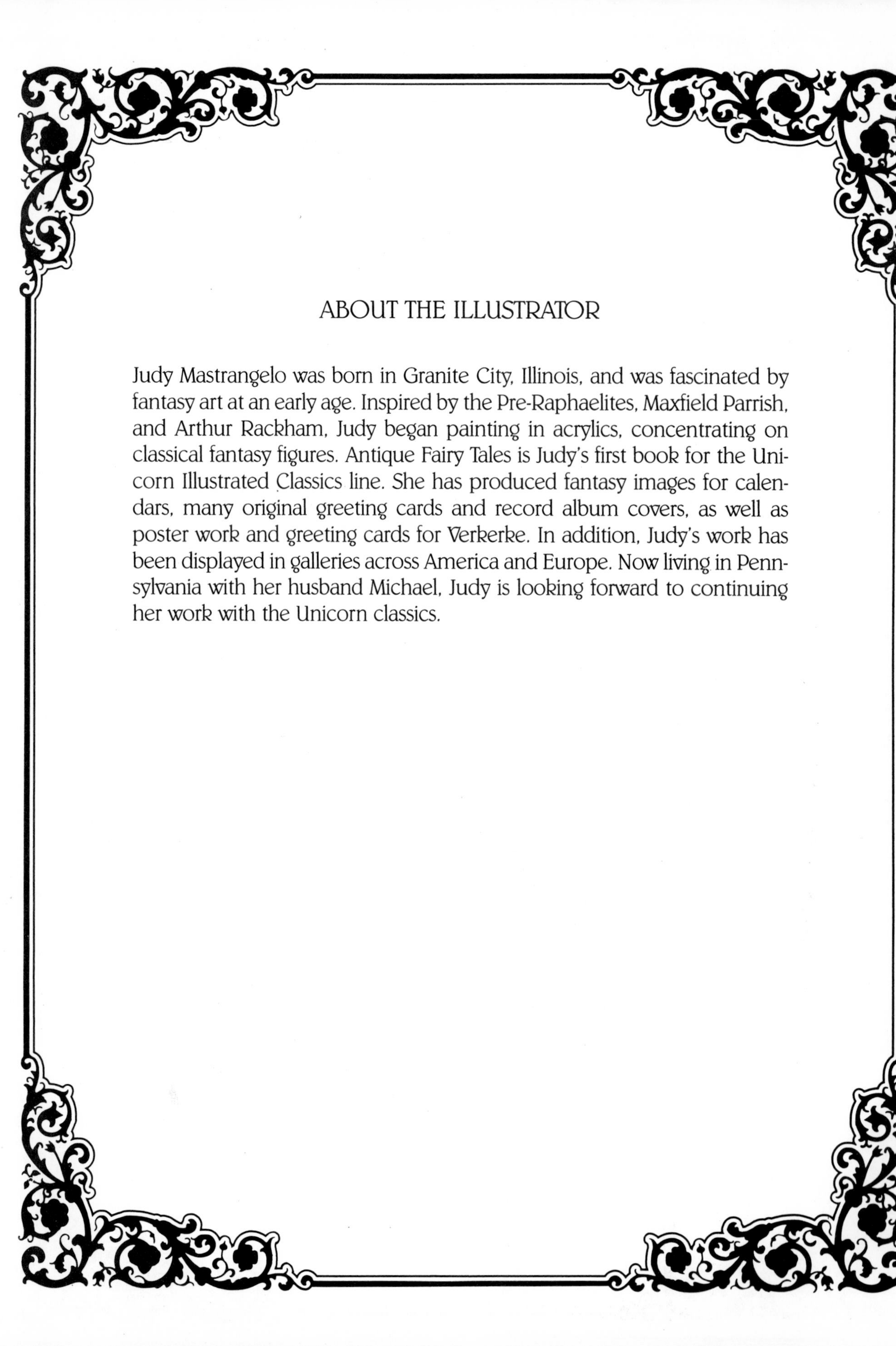

ABOUT THE ILLUSTRATOR

Judy Mastrangelo was born in Granite City, Illinois, and was fascinated by fantasy art at an early age. Inspired by the Pre-Raphaelites, Maxfield Parrish, and Arthur Rackham, Judy began painting in acrylics, concentrating on classical fantasy figures. Antique Fairy Tales is Judy's first book for the Unicorn Illustrated Classics line. She has produced fantasy images for calendars, many original greeting cards and record album covers, as well as poster work and greeting cards for Verkerke. In addition, Judy's work has been displayed in galleries across America and Europe. Now living in Pennsylvania with her husband Michael, Judy is looking forward to continuing her work with the Unicorn classics.

To my loving husband, Michael,
for all of his inspiration, patience, help and encouragement
throughout the years,
and to Bunny, our dear little friend.

Judy Mastrangelo

Illustrated By

JUDY MASTRANGELO

The Unicorn Publishing House
New Jersey

Designed and edited by Jean L. Scrocco
Associate Juvenile Editor: Heidi K. L. Corso
Printed in Korea through Creative Graphics International, Inc., New York, NY
Typography by L&B Typo of NYC, New York, NY
Reproduction Photography by The Color Wheel, New York, NY

♦ ♦ ♦ ♦ ♦

♦ ♦ ♦ ♦ ♦

♦ ♦ ♦ ♦ ♦

Distributed in Canada by Doubleday Canada, Ltd., Toronto, ON M5B 1Y3, Canada.
Distributed in the rest of the world by World Wide Media, New York, NY.

♦ ♦ ♦ ♦ ♦

Special thanks to Yoh Jinno, Joe Scrocco, Bill McGuire, Kathy Pizar, Bob Rebach, and the entire Unicorn Staff.

♦ ♦ ♦ ♦ ♦

Printing History 15 14 13 12 11 10 9 8 7 6 5 4 3 2 1

♦ ♦ ♦ ♦ ♦

Library of Congress Cataloging-in-Publication Data
Antique fairy tales.
Summary: An illustrated collection of fairy tales from all over the world, including "The Steadfast Tin Soldier," "Thumbelina," and "Bluebeard."
1. Fairy tales. [1. Fairy tales. 2. Folklore]
I. Mastrangelo, Judy, 1944- ill.
PZ8.A629 1987 398.2'1 [E] 87-10784
ISBN 0-88101-070-7

Additional Classic and Contemporary Editions
Richly Illustrated in
This Unicorn Series:

PETER PAN
PINOCCHIO
POE
THE WIZARD OF OZ
DRACULA
HEIDI
FROM TOLKIEN TO OZ
TREASURES OF CHANUKAH
A CHRISTMAS TREASURY
PETER COTTONTAIL'S SURPRISE

CAST OF CHARACTERS

Elizabeth Leube • The Little Mermaid
Audrey G. Bookspan • The Sea Witch
Mary Ivy Bayard • The Prince's Bride
Jason Lubar • Mermaid's Prince; Fatima's Brother; Egyptian Prince
Francis X. McIlhenny • The Selfish Giant
Timothy Cunningham • The Boy in the Giant's Garden
Caryn Block • Wizard's Wife; Hands
Jack Kessler • Wizard
Sarah Armour • Swan Fairy's Daughter
Judy Mastrangelo • Swan Fairy
Marcy Nguyen • Li-Ho
Tai Thai • Wang
Rose Dyer • Pandora
Timothy Tracy • Epimetheus
Kathy L. Arena • Hope; Fairy Queen
Edward Meyers • Imps; Mercury; Flower Folk
Matthew Stokes • The Angel
Michael G. Mastrangelo • Angel Boy
Willie Adler • Blue Beard
Kimberly McCartney • Fatima
Gary Gresh • Fatima's Brother
John D. Haasz • The Happy Prince; White Cat's Prince
Joel Sokoloff • Fisherman; Indian Giant
J. Frederic Trenary • The Tin Soldier; The Flower Prince
Lauren Wright • The Ballerina
Trevor Shadow • Imp
Fredi Sokoloff • Fisherman's Wife
Danielle Capriotti • Cinderella
Stephanie Wolf Spassoff • The Fairy Godmother
Michael B. Mastrangelo • King Midas
Regina Szczesniak • Marygold
Matthew Blain • Jack
Mark Fitch • Giant
Brendan Dougherty • Tippitin
Melissa Johnsson Elstien • Thumbelina
Sari Braff • Flower Folk
Lisa Collins • Flower Folk
Reiko Kimura • Flower Folk
Kurt Kramer • Flower Folk
Veronica Lynn • Flower Folk
Albert Volk • Flower Folk
Walter Wood IV • Flower Folk

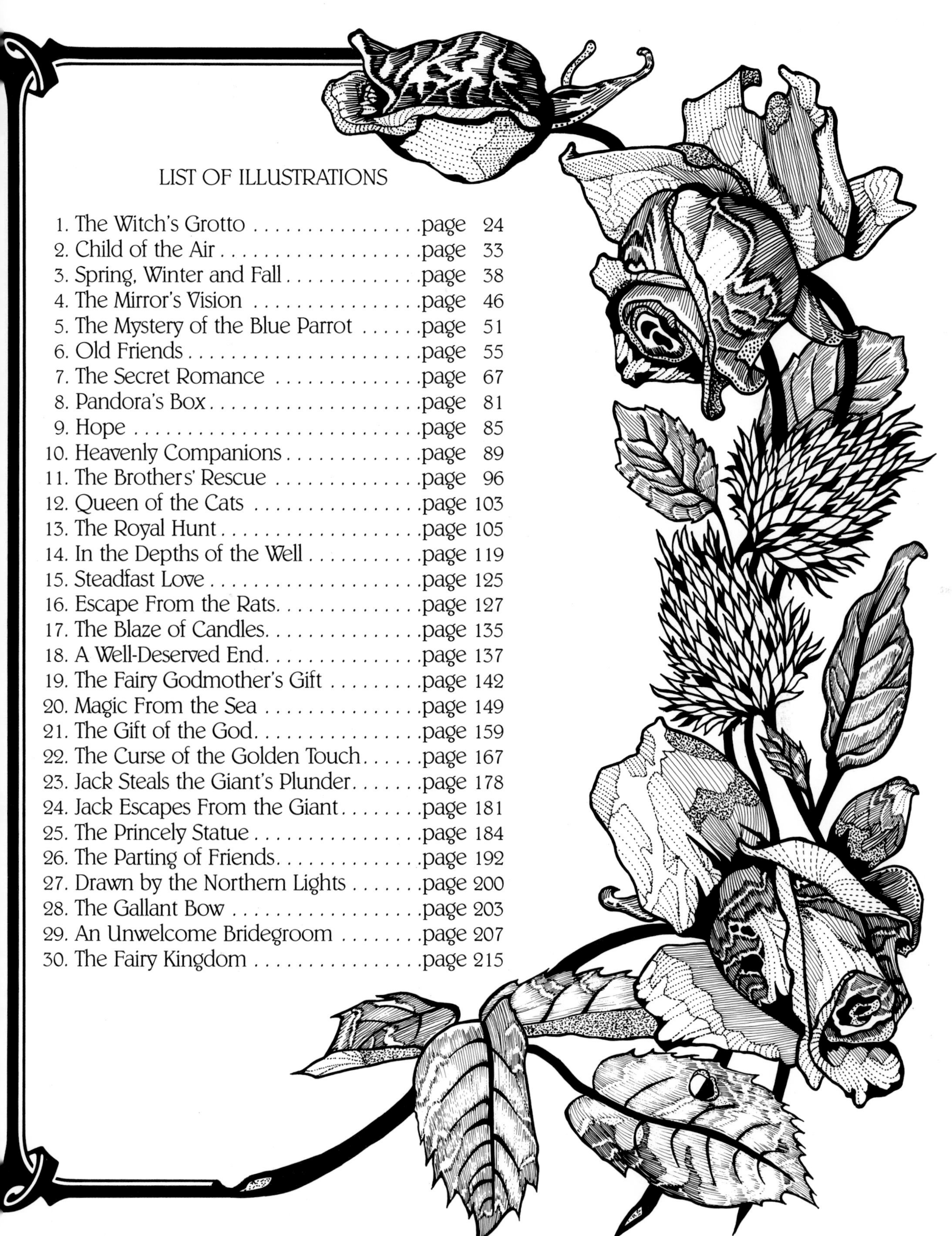

LIST OF ILLUSTRATIONS

CONTENTS

THE LITTLE MERMAID

Far out in the ocean the water is as blue as the petals of the most beautiful cornflower and as clear as the purest glass. But it is very deep — much deeper, indeed, than any cable can sound. Many steeples would have to be piled one on top of the other to reach from the bottom to the surface of the water. Down there live the sea-folk.

Now you must not think that there is nothing but the bare white sand down at the bottom. No, there grow the strangest trees and plants, with such pliable stems and leaves that at the slightest movement of the water they stir as if they were alive. All the big and little fishes glide among their branches, as the birds do up above in the air. Where the ocean is deepest stands the sea-king's palace. Its walls are made of coral, and the high arched windows are of the clearest amber. The roof is made of mussel shells, which open and close in the current. It is very beautiful, for each of them is filled with gleaming pearls, a single one of which would make a fit jewel for a queen's crown.

The sea-king had been a widower for many years, but his old mother kept house for him. She was a clever woman, but very vain of her noble rank; so she wore twelve oysters on her tail, while other grand folk were only allowed to wear six. In other respects she deserved great praise, especially for her tender care of the little sea-princesses, her granddaughters. They were six lovely children, and the youngest was the most beautiful of all. Her skin was as clear and delicate as a rose petal, and her eyes were as blue as the deepest sea, but like all the others, she had no legs — her body ended in a silvery fishtail. All day long they used to play in the great halls of the palace, where living flowers grew out of the walls. The large amber windows were thrown open, and the fishes came swimming in to them, as the swallows fly in to us when we open our windows; but the fishes swam right up to the little princesses, and ate out of their hands, and let themselves be stroked and fondled like pet canaries.

In front of the palace was a large garden, in which bright-red and dark-blue trees were growing. The fruit glittered like gold, and the flowers looked like flames of fire, with their ever-moving stems and leaves. The ground was covered with the finest sand, as blue as the flame of sulfur. A strange blue light shone over everything; one would imagine oneself to be high up in the air, with the blue sky above and below, rather than at the bottom of the sea. When the sea was calm one could see the sun; it looked like a huge purple flower, from whose center the light streamed forth.

Each of the little princesses had her own little place in the garden, where she could dig and plant as she pleased. One gave her flower bed the shape of a whale; another liked better to make hers like a little mermaid; but the youngest made hers as round as the sun and only had flowers that shone red like it. She was a strange child, quiet and thoughtful. While her sisters made a great display of all sorts of curious objects that they found from wrecked ships, she only loved her red-rose flowers, like the sun above, and a beautiful marble statue of a handsome boy, carved out of clear white stone, which had sunk from some wreck to the bottom of the sea. She had planted by the statue a rose-colored weeping willow tree, which grew well, hanging over it with its fresh branches reaching down to the blue sand and casting a violet shadow that moved to and fro like the branches, so that it seemed as if the top and the roots of the tree were playing at kissing each other.

Nothing gave her greater pleasure than to hear stories about the world of men above, and her old grandmother had to tell her all she knew about ships and towns, men and animals. It seemed strangely beautiful to her that on earth the flowers were fragrant — for at the bottom of the sea they have no scent — and that the woods were green, and that the fish that one saw there among the branches could sing so loudly and beautifully that it was a delight to hear them. The grandmother called the little birds fishes; otherwise her granddaughter would not have understood her, as they had never seen a bird.

"When you are fifteen years old," said the grandmother, "you will be allowed to rise up to the surface of the sea and sit on the rocks in the moonlight, and see the big ships as they sail by. Then you will also see the forests and towns."

The following year one of the sisters would be fifteen; but the others — well, the sisters were each one year younger than the other; so the youngest had to wait fully five years before she could come up from the bottom of the sea and see what things were like on the earth above. But each promised to tell her sisters what she had seen and liked best for her first day; for their grandmother could not tell them enough — there were so many things about which they wanted to know. None of them, however, longed so much to go up as the youngest, who had the longest time to wait, and was so quiet and thoughtful. Many a night she stood at the open window and looked up through the dark-blue water, where the fishes splashed with their fins and tails. She could see the moon and the stars, which only shone faintly, but looked much bigger through the water than we see them. When something like a dark cloud passed under them and hid them for a while, she knew it was either a whale swimming overhead or a ship with many people, who had no idea that a lovely little mermaid was standing below stretching out her white hands toward the keel of their ship.

The eldest princess was now fifteen years old and was allowed to rise to the surface of the sea. When she came back she had hundreds of things to tell. But what pleased her most, she said, was to lie in the moonlight on a sandbank, in the calm sea, and to see near the coast the big town where the lights twinkled like many hundreds of stars; to hear music and the noise and bustle of carriages and people; and to see the many church towers and spires and listen to the ringing of the bells. Oh, how the youngest sister listened to all this! And when, later on in the evening, she again stood at the open window, looking up through the dark-blue water, she thought of the big town, with all its bustle and noise, and imagined she could hear the church bells ringing, even down where she was.

The year after, the second sister was allowed to go up to the surface, and swim about as she pleased. She came up just as the sun was setting, and this sight she thought the most beautiful of all she saw. The whole sky was like gold, she said, and the clouds — well, she could not find words to describe their loveliness. Rose and violet, they sailed by over her head; but, even swifter than the clouds, a flock of wild swans, like a long white veil, flew across the water toward the sun. She followed them, but the sun sank, and the rosy gleam faded from the sea and clouds.

The year after, the third sister went up. She was the boldest of them all and swam up a broad river that flowed into the sea. She saw beautiful green hills covered with vines, and houses and castles peeped out from magnificent woods. She heard the birds sing, and the sun shone so warmly that she often had to dive under the water to cool her burning face. In a little creek she came across a whole flock of little children, who were quite naked and splashed about in the water; she wanted to play with them, but they ran away terrified. Then a little black animal — it was a dog, but she had never seen a dog before — came out and barked so ferociously at her that she was frightened and hurried back as fast as she could to the open sea. But she could never forget the magnificent woods, the green hills, and the lovely children, who could swim even though they had no fishtails.

The fourth sister was not so daring; she stayed far out in the open sea and said that that was the loveliest place off all. There, she said, one could see for many miles around, and the sky above was like a great glass dome. She saw ships, but far away, and they looked to her like seagulls. The playful dolphins, she said, turned somersaults, and the big whales spouted out seawater through their nostrils, as if a hundred fountains were playing all around her.

Now the fifth sister's turn came, and as her birthday was in the winter, she saw on her first visit things the other sisters had not. The sea looked quite green; huge icebergs floated around her — they were like pearls, she said, and yet were much higher than the church steeples built by men. They were the strangest shapes and glittered like diamonds. She sat on one of the biggest, and all the passing sailors were terrified when they saw her sitting there, with the wind playing with her long hair. But toward evening the sky became overcast with black clouds; there was thunder and lightning, and the dark waves lifted up the big blocks of ice, which shone in each flash of lightning. On all the ships the sails were reefed, and there was anxiety and terror; but she sat quietly on her floating iceberg and watched the blue lightning dart in zigzags into the foaming sea.

The first time each one of the sisters came to the surface, all the new and beautiful things she saw charmed her. But now, when as grown-up girls they were allowed to come up whenever they liked, they became indifferent to them, longing for their home; and after a month they said that after all it was best down below, where one felt at home. On many an evening the five sisters would rise to the surface of the sea, arm in arm. They had beautiful voices, far finer than that of any human being; and when a storm was brewing, and they thought that some ships might be wrecked, they swam in front of them, singing beautifully of how lovely it was at the bottom of the sea and telling the people not to be afraid of coming down there. But the human beings could not understand the words and thought it was only the noise of the storm; and they never saw the wonders down below, for when the ship went down they were drowned and were dead when they came to the sea-king's palace. When her sisters went up arm and arm to the top of the sea there stood the little sister, all alone, looking after them and feeling as if she could cry; but mermaids have no tears, and so they suffer all the more.

"Oh, if only I were fifteen!" she said. "I know how much I shall love the world above, and the people who live in it."

At last she was fifteen years old.

"Well, now we have you off our hands," said her grandmother, the old dowager queen. "Come now! Let me adorn you like your other sisters!" She put a wreath of white lilies on her head, but every petal of the flowers was half a pearl; and the old lady had eight big oysters fixed to the princess's tail, to show her high rank.

"But it hurts so!" said the little mermaid.

"Yes, one must suffer to be beautiful," the old lady replied.

Oh, how gladly the little princess would have taken off all her ornaments and the heavy wreath! The red flowers in her garden would have suited her much better, but she dared not make any changes now. "Good-bye!" she said and rose as lightly as a bubble through the water.

The sun had just set when she lifted her head out of the water, but the clouds gleamed with red and gold, and the evening star shone in the rosy sky. The air was mild and fresh, and the sea as calm as glass. Near her lay a big ship with three masts; only one sail was set, as not a breath of wind was stirring, and the sailors were sitting about on deck and in the rigging. There was music and singing onboard, and when it grew dark many hundreds of colored lamps were lighted, and it looked as if the flags of all nations were floating in the air. The little mermaid swam up close to the cabin windows, and when the waves lifted her up she could see through the clear panes many richly dressed people. But the handsomest of them all was the young prince, with large black eyes — he could not have been older than sixteen; and it was his birthday that was the reason for all this celebration. The sailors were dancing on deck, and when the young prince came out, hundreds of rockets were sent off into the air, making the night as bright as day. The little mermaid was frightened and dived underwater. But soon she lifted up her head again, and then it seemed to her as if all the stars of heaven were falling down upon her. Never had she seen such fireworks! Great suns whirled around, gorgeous fiery fish flew through the blue air, and everything was reflected in the calm and glassy sea. The ship was so brilliantly lighted up that one could see everything distinctly, even to the smallest rope, and the people still better. Oh, how beautiful was the young prince! He shook hands with the people and smiled graciously, while the music sounded dreamily through the starry night.

It grew very late, but the little mermaid could not turn her eyes away from the ship and the handsome prince. The colored lamps were put out, no more rockets were sent off nor cannons fired. But deep down in the sea was a strange moaning and murmuring, and the little mermaid sitting on the waves was rocked up and down, so that she could look into the cabin. Soon the ship began to make greater headway, as one sail after another was unfurled. Then the waves rose higher and higher; dark clouds gathered; and flashes of lightning were seen in the distance. Oh, what a terrible storm was brewing! Then the sailors reefed all the sails, and the big ship rushed at flying speed through the wild sea. The waves rose as high as great black mountains, as if they would dash over the masts, but the ship dived like a swan between them, and then was carried up again to their towering crests. The little mermaid thought this was great fun; but not so the sailors. The ship creaked and groaned, her strong timbers bending under the weight of the huge waves. The sea broke over her; the mainmast snapped in two, like a reed; and the ship lay over on her side while the water rushed into her hold. The little mermaid then realized that the crew was in danger; she herself had to be careful of the beams and planks floating about in the water. For one moment it was so dark that not a thing could be seen, but flashes of lightning made everything visible, and she could see all on board. The little mermaid looked out for the young prince, and as the ship broke up she saw him sinking into the deep sea. At first she was very pleased, for now he would come down to her; but then she remembered that men cannot live in the water, and only if he were dead could he come to her father's palace. No, he must not die! Heedless of the beams and planks floating on the water, which might have crushed her, she dived down into the water and came up again in the waves, in search of the prince. At last she found him. His strength was failing him, and he could hardly swim any longer in the stormy sea; his arms and legs began to grown numb and his beautiful eyes closed; he would certainly have died if the little mermaid had not come to his assistance. She held his head above water and let the waves carry them where they would.

Next morning the storm was over, but not a plank of the ship was anywhere to be seen. The sun rose red and brilliant out of the water, and seemed to bring new life to the prince's cheeks; but his eyes remained closed. The little mermaid kissed his beautiful high forehead, and smoothed back his wet hair; she thought he looked very much like the white marble statue in her little garden. She kissed him again and again, and prayed that he might live.

Then she saw before her eyes the mainland, where lay high, blue mountains on whose summits snow was glistening, so that they looked like swans. Down by the shore were beautiful green woods, and in front of them stood a church or convent — she did not know which, but it was some sort of building. Lemon trees and orange trees grew in the garden, and before the gate stood lofty palm trees. The sea formed a little bay here and was quite calm, though very deep. She swam straight to the cliffs, where the fine white sand had been washed ashore, and laid the handsome prince on the sand, taking special care that his head lay raised up in the warm sunshine. Then all the bells began to ring in the big white building, and many young girls came out into the garden. The little mermaid swam farther out and hid behind some rocks, covering her hair and breast with sea-foam, lest anybody should see her little face; and from there she watched to see who would come to the poor prince.

It was not long before a young girl came to the spot where he lay. At first she seemed very frightened, but only for a moment, and then she called some of the others. The little mermaid saw that the prince came back to life and smiled at all who stood around him; but at her he did not smile — he little knew who had saved him. She was very sad; and when they had taken him into the big building she dived sorrowfully down into the water, and so went back to her father's palace.

She had always been silent and thoughtful, and now she became still more so. Her sisters asked her what she had seen when she went up for the first time, but she told them nothing. Many a morning and many an evening she went back to the place where she had left the prince. She saw how the fruit in the garden ripened and was gathered, and how the snow melted on the high mountains, but she never saw the prince; and each time she returned home she was more sorrowful than before.

Her only comfort was to sit in her little garden and put her arms around the marble figure that was so like the prince. But she no longer looked after her flowers; her garden became a wilderness: the plants straggled over the paths and twined their long stalks and leaves around the branches of trees, so that it became quite dark there.

At last she could bear the burden of her sorrow no longer and confided her troubles to one of her sisters, who, of course, told the others. These and a few other mermaids, who also told their intimate friends, were the only people in the whole of the ocean world who were in on the secret. One of them knew who the prince was and could tell them where his kingdom lay. She also had watched the festivities on board the ship.

"Come, little sister!" said the other princesses, and arm in arm, in a long row, they rose to the surface of the sea, in front of where the prince's palace stood. It was built of bright-yellow stone and had broad marble staircases, one of which reached right down to the sea. Magnificent gilt cupolas surmounted the roof, and in the colonnades, which ran all around the building, stood lifelike marble statues. Through the clear panes of the high windows could be seen splendid halls, hung with costly silk curtains and beautiful tapestries, and on all the walls were paintings that were a joy to look at. In the center of the largest hall a big fountain was playing. Its jets rose as high as the glass dome in the ceiling, through which the sun shone on the water and on the beautiful plants that grew in the great basin.

Now she knew where he lived and came there many an evening and many a night across the water. She swam much closer to the shore than any of the others would have ventured, and she even went up the narrow channel under the magnificent marble terrace, which cast a long shadow over the water. Here she would sit and gaze at the young prince, who thought that he was all alone in the bright moonlight.

Many an evening she saw him sailing in his stately boat, with music on board and flags waving. She watched from behind the green rushes, and when the wind caught her long silvery-white veil, and people saw it, they thought it was a swan spreading its wings. Many a night when the fishermen were out at sea fishing by torchlight she heard them say many good things about the prince, and she was glad that she had saved his life when he was drifting half-dead upon the waves. She remembered how heavily his head had lain upon her breast and how passionately she had kissed him, but he knew nothing about it and did not even see her in his dreams.

More and more she grew to love the human beings, and more and more she longed to be able to live among them, for their world seemed to her so much bigger than hers. They could sail over the sea in great ships and climb mountains high above the clouds, and the lands that they owned stretched, in woods and fields, farther than her eyes could see. There were still so many things she wanted to know about, and her sisters could not answer all her questions; so she asked her grandmother, who knew the upper world very well, and rightly called it "the countries above the sea."

"If human beings are not drowned," asked the little mermaid, "can they live forever and ever? Don't they die as we do down here in the sea?"

"Yes," the old lady replied, "they also die, and their lives are even shorter than ours. We can live to be three hundred years old, but when we cease to exist we are turned into foam on the water, and have not even a grave down here among our dear ones. We are like the green rushes, which, when once cut down, can never grow again. Human beings, however, have a soul which lives forever, lives even after the body has become dust; it rises through the clear air up to the shining stars. As we rise out of the water and see all the countries of the earth, so they rise to unknown, beautiful regions which we shall never see."

"Why don't we also have an immortal soul?" asked the little mermaid sorrowfully. "I would gladly give all the hundreds of years I have yet to live if I could only be a human being for one day, and afterward have a share in the heavenly kingdom."

"You must not think about that," said the old lady. "We are much happier and better off than the human beings up there."

"So I must die, and float as foam on the sea, and never hear the music of the waves or see the beautiful flowers and the red sun! Is there nothing I can do to win an immortal soul?"

"No," the grandmother said. "Only if a man loved you so much that you were dearer to him than father or mother, and if he clung to you with all his heart and all his love, and let the priest place his right hand in yours, with the promise to be faithful to you here and to eternity — then would his soul flow into your body, and you would receive a share in the happiness of mankind. He would give you a soul and yet still keep his own. But that can never happen! What is thought most beautiful here below, your fishtail, they would consider ugly on earth — they do not know any better. Up there one must have two clumsy supports, which they call legs, in order to be beautiful."

The little mermaid sighed and looked sadly at her fishtail.

"Let us be happy!" said the old lady. "Let us hop and skip through the three hundred years of our life! That is surely long enough! And afterward we can rest all the better in our graves. This evening there is to be a court ball."

Such a splendid sight has never been seen on earth. The walls and ceiling of the big ballroom were of thick but transparent glass. Several hundred colossal mussel shells, red and grass-green, stood in rows down the sides, holding blue flames that illuminated the whole room and shone through the walls, so that the sea outside was brightly lit up. One could see innumerable fish, both big and small, swimming outside the glass walls; some with gleaming purple scales and others glittering like silver and gold. Through the middle of the ballroom flowed a broad stream, in which the mermen and mermaids danced to their own beautiful singing. No human beings have such lovely voices. The little mermaid sang most sweetly of all, and they all applauded her. For a moment she felt joyful at heart at the thought that she had the most beautiful voice on land or in the sea; but soon her mind returned to the world above, for she could not forget the handsome prince and her sorrow at not possessing an immortal soul like his. So she stole out of her father's palace, while all within was joy and merriment, and sat sorrowfully in her little garden.

Suddenly she heard the sound of a horn through the water, and she thought: Now he is sailing above, he whom I love more than father or mother, and into whose hands I would entrust my life's happiness. I will dare anything to win him and an immortal soul. While my sisters are dancing in my father's palace I will go to the sea-witch, whom I have always feared so much. Perhaps she may be able to give me advice and help.

Then the little mermaid left her garden and went out toward the roaring whirlpools where the witch lived. She had never been that way before; neither flowers nor seaweed grew there — only bare, gray sand stretching to the whirlpools, where the water swirled around like rushing mill wheels, dragging everything it got hold of down into the depths. She had to pass right through these dreadful whirlpools to reach the witch's territory. For a long way the only path led over bubbling mud, which the witch called the peat bog. Behind this her house stood, in a strange forest, for all the trees and bushes were polyps — half animals and half plants — which looked like hundred-headed snakes growing out of the ground. All the branches were slimy arms with fingers like wriggling worms, and they moved joint by joint from the root to the topmost branch. Everything that they could lay hold of in the sea they clutched and held fast, and never let go again. The little mermaid stopped timidly in front of them. Her heart was beating with fear, and she nearly turned back; but then she thought of the prince and man's immortal soul, and took courage. She twisted her long flowing hair around her head, in case the polyps should seize her by it, and, crossing her hands on her breast, she darted through the water as fast as a fish, right past the hideous polyps, who stretched out their writhing arms and fingers after her. She saw that each one of them had seized something and held it tightly with hundreds of little arms like bands of iron. The bleached bones of men who had perished at sea and sunk into the depths were tightly grasped in the arms of some, while others clutched ship's rudders and sea chests, skeletons of land animals, and a little mermaid whom they had caught and strangled, which was the most terrifying sight of all to her.

She now came to a big marshy place in the forest, where big, fat water snakes were writhing about, showing their ugly yellow bellies. In the middle of this place stood a house built of the white bones of ship-wrecked men, and there sat the sea-witch, letting a toad eat out of her mouth, as we should feed a little canary with sugar. The ugly, fat water snakes she called

her little chickens, and she allowed them to crawl all over her hideous bosom.

"I know quite well what you want!" said the sea-witch. "It is silly of you! But you shall have your way, for it is sure to bring you misfortune, my pretty princess! You want to get rid of your fishtail and have instead two stumps which human beings use for walking, so that the young prince may fall in love with you, and you may win him and an immortal soul!" As she said this the old witch laughed so loudly and horribly that the toad and the snakes fell to the ground, where they crawled about. "You have only just come in time," said the witch, "for if you had come after sunrise tomorrow I should not have been able to help you till another year had passed. I will make you a drink, and before sunrise you must swim ashore and sit on the beach and drink it. Then your tail will split in two and shrink into what human beings call legs; but it will hurt you, as if a sharp sword were running through you. Every one who sees you will say that you are the most beautiful child of man they have ever seen. You will keep your gracefulness, and no dancer will be able to move as lightly as you; but at each step you take you will feel as if you were treading on a sharp knife, and as if your blood must flow. Are you willing to suffer all this, and shall I help you?"

"Yes," said the little mermaid in a trembling voice, and she thought of the prince and of winning an immortal soul.

"But remember!" the witch said. "When once you have taken the human form you can never become a mermaid again. You will never again be able to dive down through the water to your sisters and your father's palace. And if you fail to win the prince's love, so that for your sake he will forget father and mother, and cling to you with body and soul, and make the priest join your hands as man and wife, you will not be given an immortal soul. On the first morning after he has married another your heart will break, and you will turn into foam on the water."

"I will do it," said the little mermaid, as pale as death.

"But you will have to pay me," the witch said, "and it is not a trifle that I ask. You have the most beautiful voice of all who live at the bottom of the sea, with which you probably think you can enchant the prince; but this voice you must give to me. I must have the best thing you possess in return for my precious drink, for I have to give you my own blood in it, so that the drink may be as sharp as a two-edged sword."

"But if you take away my voice," said the little mermaid, "what have I got left?"

"Your lovely figure," the witch replied, "your grace of movement, and your speaking eyes! With these surely you can capture a human heart. Well, have you lost your courage? Put out your little tongue, so that I may cut if off in payment, and you shall have the powerful drink."

"Do it," said the little mermaid, and the witch put her caldron on the fire to prepare the magic drink. "Cleanliness is a good thing," she said, and scoured the caldron with snakes that she had tied into a bundle. Then she pricked her breast and let her black blood drip into it, and the steam rose up in the weirdest shapes, so that one could not help being frightened and horrified. Every moment the witch threw some new thing into the caldron, and when it boiled the sound was like crocodiles weeping. At last the drink was ready, and it looked like the clearest water.

"Here it is!" said the witch, and she cut off the little mermaid's tongue, so that now she was dumb and could neither sing nor speak. "If the polyps should catch hold of you when you go back through my wood," the witch said, "you need only throw one drop of this liquid over them, and their arms and fingers will fly into a thousand pieces!" But the little mermaid had no need to do this, for the polyps shrank back from her in terror at the sight of the sparkling drink, which gleamed in her hand like a glittering star. So she came quickly through the forest and the bog and roaring whirlpools.

She could see her father's palace: in the ballroom the lamps were all darkened, and every one was asleep; but she dared not go in to them, now that she was dumb and about to leave them forever. She felt as if her heart would break with sorrow. She stole into the garden, took a flower from each of her sister's flower beds, kissed her hand a thousand times to the palace, and swam up through the dark-blue sea.

The sun had not yet risen when she came in sight of the prince's palace and reached the magnificent marble steps. The moon was shining bright and clear. The little mermaid drank the sharp, burning draft, and it felt as if a two-edged sword went through her tender body; she fainted and lay as if dead.

When the sun shone over the sea she awoke and felt a stabbing pain; but there before her stood the beautiful young prince. He fixed his black eyes on her, so that she cast hers down, and then she saw that her fishtail had disappeared and that she had the prettiest little white legs that any girl could possess. But she was quite naked, so she wrapped herself in her long thick hair. The prince asked her who she was and how she came there, and she looked at him tenderly and yet sadly with her deep-blue eyes, for she could not speak. Then he took her by the hand and led her into the palace. Every step she took felt, as the witch had warned her, as if she were trodding on pointed needles and sharp knives, but she bore it gladly and walked as lightly as a soap bubble by the side of the prince, who, with all the others, admired her grace of movement.

She was given wonderful dresses of silk and muslin to put on, and she was the greatest beauty in the palace; but she was dumb and unable either to sing or speak. Beautiful slaves, dressed in silk and gold, came to sing before the prince and his royal parents. One of them sang better than all the rest, and the prince clapped his hands and smiled at her. Then the little mermaid grew sad, for she knew that she had been able to sing far more beautifully; and she thought: Oh, if he only knew that to be with him I have given away my voice forever!

Now the slaves began to dance light, graceful dances to the loveliest music; and then the little mermaid lifted her beautiful white arms, rose on her toes, and glided across the floor, dancing as none of the others had danced. At every movement her beauty seemed to grow, and her eyes spoke more deeply to the heart than the songs of the slave girls. Everyone was charmed by her, especially the prince, who called her his little foundling, and she danced again and again, although every time her feet touched the ground she felt as if she were treading on sharp knives. The prince said that she should always be near him, and let her sleep on a velvet cushion before his door.

He had a man's dress made for her, so that she might ride with him. They rode through fragrant woods, where the green branches brushed her shoulders and the little birds sang among the fresh leaves. She climbed with the prince up the high mountains, and, though her tender feet bled so that even others could see it, she smiled and followed him, till they saw the clouds sailing beneath their feet, like a flock of birds flying to foreign lands.

At home, in the prince's palace, when all the others were asleep in their beds at night, she would go out onto the marble steps. It cooled her burning feet to stand in the cold seawater, and then she thought of times past and of those she had left far down below in the deep.

One night her sisters came up arm in arm, singing sorrowfully as they swam through the water, and she beckoned to them; they recognized her and told her how sad she had made them all. After that they came to see her every night, and one night she saw far out her old grandmother, who had not been up to the surface for many, many years, and the sea-king, with his crown on his head. They stretched out their hands toward her but did not venture as close to land as her sisters.

Day by day the prince grew fonder of her; he loved her as one would love a good, sweet child, but he never had the slightest idea of making her his queen. Yet his wife she must be, or she could not win an immortal soul, but on his wedding morning would turn into foam on the sea.

"Don't you love me more than them all?" the little mermaid's eyes seemed to say when the prince took her in his arms and kissed her beautiful forehead.

"Yes, you are the dearest to me," he said, "for you have the best heart of them all. You are the most devoted to me, and you are like a young girl whom I once saw, but whom I fear I shall never meet again. I was on board a ship which was wrecked, and the waves washed me ashore near a holy temple where several young maidens were serving in attendance. The youngest of them found me on the beach and saved my life. I only saw her twice. She is the only girl in the world I could love, but you are like her, and you almost drive her image from my heart. She belongs to the holy temple, and so by good fortune you have been sent to me, and we shall never be parted."

Alas! He doesn't know that it was I who saved his life! thought the little mermaid. I carried him across the sea to the wood where the temple stands; and I was hidden in the foam, watching to see if anyone would come to him. I saw the beautiful girl whom he loves better than me. She sighed deeply, for she could not weep. The girl belongs to the holy temple, he said. She will never come out into the world, and they will never meet again; but I am with him, and see him every day. I will care for him, love him, and give up my life for him.

But soon the rumor spread that the prince was to marry the beautiful daughter of a neighboring king, and that that was why they were fitting up such a magnificent ship. The prince is going to visit the neighboring king's country, they said, but really he is going to see his daughter, and a large suite is to accompany him. The little mermaid shook her head and smiled, for she knew the prince's thoughts much better than the others. "I must go," he said to her. "I must see the beautiful princess, for my parents wish it; but they will not force me to bring her home as my bride. I cannot love her. She will not be like the beautiful girl in the temple whom you are like. If one day I were to choose a bride I would rather have you, my dumb foundling with the eloquent eyes." And he kissed her red lips, played with her long hair, and laid his head on her heart, so that she began to dream of human happiness and an immortal soul.

"You are not afraid of the sea, my dumb child?" he said to her, when they were standing on board the stately ship that was to carry him to the neighboring king's country. He told her of the storm and of the calm, of the strange fish in the deep, and of the marvelous things that divers had seen down there. She smiled at his words, for she knew more about the things at the bottom of the sea than anyone else.

At night, in the moonlight, when all were asleep except the man at the helm, she sat by the ship's rail, gazing down into the clear water, and thought she could see her father's palace, and her grandmother, with her silver crown on her head, looking up through the swirling currents at the ship's keel. Then her sisters came up out of the water, looking sorrowfully at her and wringing their white hands. She beckoned to them and smiled, and wanted to tell them that she was well and happy, but a cabin boy came up to her, and her sisters dived under, so that he thought the white things he had seen were just foam on the sea.

The next morning the ship reached the harbor of the neighboring king's magnificent city. All the church bells were ringing, and from the high towers trumpets sounded, while soldiers paraded with flying colors and glittering bayonets. Every day there were festivities; balls and receptions followed one another. But the princess had not yet arrived. She was being brought up in a holy convent far away, they said, where she was learning every royal virtue. At last she came. The little mermaid was anxious to see her beauty, and she had to admit that she had never seen a lovelier being: her skin was clear and delicate, and behind her long dark lashes smiled a pair of deep-blue, loyal eyes.

"You are she!" said the prince. "She who saved me when I lay almost dead on the shore!" And he clasped his blushing bride in his arms.

"Oh, I am too happy!" he said to the little mermaid. "My greatest wish, which I have never dared to hope for, has come true. You will rejoice at my happiness, for you love me more than them all." The little mermaid kissed his hand and felt as if her heart were already breaking. His wedding morning, she knew, would bring death to her, and she would turn into foam on the sea.

The church bells pealed, and heralds rode through the streets announcing the betrothal. On all the altars sweet-smelling oil was burning in costly silver lamps. The priests swung their censers, and the bride and bridegroom joined hands and received the bishop's blessing. The little mermaid, dressed in silk and gold, stood holding the bride's train, but her ears did not hear the joyous music, and her eyes saw nothing of the sacred ceremony — she was thinking of the night of her death, and of all that she had lost in this world.

That same evening the bride and bridegroom came on board the ship; cannons roared, flags were waving, and in the middle of the ship was erected a royal tent of purple and gold, with the most magnificent couch, where the bridal pair were to rest through the still, cool night.

The sails swelled in the wind, and the ship glided smoothly and almost without motion over the clear sea. When it grew dark, colored lamps were lighted, and the sailors danced merrily on deck. The little mermaid could not help thinking of the first time she had risen to the surface and had seen the same splendor and revelry. She threw herself among the dancers, darting and turning as a swallow turns when it is pursued, and they all applauded her, for she had never danced so wonderfully before. It was like sharp knives cutting her tender feet, but she did not feel it, for the pain in her heart was much greater. She knew that it was the last evening that she would be with him — him for whom she had left her family and her home, sacrificed her lovely voice, and daily suffered endless pain, of which he had not the slightest idea. It was the last night that she would breathe the same air as he, and see the deep sea and the starry sky. An unending night, without thoughts or dreams, was waiting for her, who had no soul and could not win one. On board the ship the rejoicing and revelry lasted till long past midnight, and she laughed and danced with the thought of death in her heart. The prince kissed his beautiful bride, and she played with his dark hair, and arm in arm they retired to rest in the magnificent tent.

Then everything grew quiet on board; only the steersman stood at the helm, and the little mermaid laid her white arms on the rail and looked toward the east for the rosy glimmer of dawn, for she knew that the first sunbeam would kill her.

Then she saw her sisters rising out of the waves; they were as pale as she was, and their beautiful hair no longer floated in the wind, for it had been cut off. "We have given it to the witch, to get her help, so that you need not die tonight. She has given us a knife: here it is. See how sharp it is! Before the sun rises you must thrust it into prince's heart, and when the warm blood sprinkles your feet they will grow together again into a fishtail. Then you will be a mermaid again, and you can come down with us into the sea, and live your three hundred years before you turn into dead salt sea-foam. Hurry! For he or you must die before sunrise. Our old grandmother is so full of grief for you that her white hair has all fallen off, as ours fell under the witch's scissors. Kill the prince and come back to us! Hurry! Do you see that red streak in the sky? In a few moments the sun will rise, and then you must die!" They gave a deep sigh and disappeared beneath the waves.

The little mermaid drew back the purple curtain of the tent and saw the lovely bride lying asleep with her head on the prince's breast, and she bent down and kissed him on his beautiful forehead. She looked up at the sky, where the rosy glow was growing brighter and brighter, and then at the sharp knife, and again at the prince, who murmured his bride's name in his dreams. Yes, she alone was in his thoughts, and for a moment the knife trembled in the little mermaid's hand. But suddenly she flung it far out into the waves, which shone red where it fell, so that it looked as if drops of blood were splashing up out of the water. Once more she looked with dimmed eyes at the prince, then she threw herself from the ship into the sea and felt her body dissolving into foam.

Now the sun rose out of the sea, and its rays fell with gentleness and warmth on the deathly cold sea-foam, and the little mermaid felt no pain of death. She saw the bright sun and, floating above her, hundreds of beautiful transparent beings, through whom she could see the white sails of the ship and the red clouds in the sky. Their voices were melodious, but so ethereal that no human ear could hear them, just as no earthly eye could see them, and without wings they floated through the air. The little mermaid saw that she had a body like theirs and was slowly rising up out of the foam.

"Where am I going to?" she asked, and her voice sounded like that of the other spirits — so ethereal that no earthly music was like it.

"To the daughters of the air," answered the others. "Mermaids have no immortal soul, and can never have one unless they win the love of a human being. Their eternal life must depend on the power of another. The daughters of the air have no immortal soul either, but by their own good deeds they can win one for themselves. We fly to the hot countries where the pestilent winds kill the human beings, and we bring them cool breezes. We spread the fragrance of flowers through the air, and bring life and healing. When for three hundred years we have striven to do all the good we can we are given an immortal soul, and share the eternal happiness of mankind. You, poor little mermaid, have struggled with all your heart for the same goal, and have suffered and endured. Now you have risen to the spiritual world, and after three hundred years of good deeds you will win an immortal soul for yourself."

And the little mermaid lifted her eyes to the sun, and for the first time she felt tears in them.

On the ship there was life and noise once more. She saw the prince and his beautiful bride looking for her, gazing sadly at the gleaming foam as if they knew that she had thrown herself into the waves. Unseen, she kissed the bride's forehead and smiled at the prince. Then she rose with the other children of the air up to the rosy clouds that sailed across the sky.

"In three hundred years we shall float like this into the kingdom of God!"

"But we may get there sooner!" whispered one of them. "Unseen, we fly into houses where there are children, and for every day on which we find a good child that gives its parents joy and deserves their love, God shortens our time of probation. The child does not know when we fly through the room, and if we smile for joy one of the three hundred years is taken off; but if we see a naughty and wicked child we must shed tears of sorrow, and every tear adds a day to our time of probation."

THE SELFISH GIANT

Every afternoon, as they were coming from school, the children used to go and play in the Giant's garden.

It was a large lovely garden, with soft green grass. Here and there over the grass stood beautiful flowers like stars, and there were twelve peach trees that in the springtime broke out into delicate blossoms of pink and pearl, and in the autumn bore rich fruit. The birds sat on the trees and sang so sweetly that the children used to stop their games in order to listen to them. "How happy we are here!" they cried to each other.

One day the Giant came back. He had been to visit his friend the Cornish ogre, and had stayed with him for seven years. After the seven years were over he had said all that he had to say, for his conversation was limited, and he determined to return to his own castle. When he arrived he saw the children playing in the garden.

"What are you doing there?" he cried in a very gruff voice, and the children ran away.

"My own garden is my own garden," said the Giant; "any one can understand that, and I will allow nobody to play in it but myself." So he built a high wall all round it, and put up a notice-board:

TRESPASSERS
WILL BE
PROSECUTED

He was a very selfish giant.

The poor children had now nowhere to play. They tried to play on the road, but the road was very dusty and full of hard stones, and they did not like it. They used to wander round the high wall when their lessons were over, and talk about the beautiful garden inside. "How happy we were there," they said to each other.

Then the Spring came, and all over the country there were little blossoms and little birds. Only in the garden of the Selfish Giant it was still winter. The birds did not care to sing in it, as there were no children, and the trees forgot to blossom. Once a beautiful flower put its head out from the grass, but when it saw the notice-board it was so sorry for the children that it slipped back into the ground again, and went off to sleep. The only people who were pleased were the Snow and the Frost. "Spring has forgotten this garden," they cried, "so we will live here all the year round." The Snow covered up the grass with her great white cloak, and the Frost painted all the trees silver. Then they invited the North Wind to stay with them, and he came. He was wrapped in furs, and he roared all day about the garden, and blew the chimney-pots down. "This is a delightful spot," he said; "we must ask the Hail on a visit." So the Hail came. Every day for three hours he rattled on the roof of the castle till he broke most of the slates, and then he ran round and round the garden as fast as he could go. He was dressed in grey, and his breath was like ice.

"I cannot understand why the Spring is so late in coming," said the Selfish Giant, as he sat at the window and looked out at his cold white garden; "I hope there will be a change in the weather."

But the Spring never came, nor the Summer. The Autumn gave golden fruit to every garden, but to the Giant's garden she gave none. "He is too selfish," she said. So it was always Winter there, and the North Wind, and the Hail, and the Frost, and the Snow danced about through the trees.

One morning the Giant was lying awake in bed when he heard some lovely music. It sounded so sweet to his ears that he thought it must be the King's musicians passing by. It was really only a little linnet singing outside his window, but it was so long since he had heard a bird sing in his garden that it seemed to him to be the most beautiful music in the world. Then the Hail stopped dancing over his head, and the North Wind ceased roaring, and a delicious perfume came to him through the open casement. "I believe the Spring has come at last," said the Giant, and he jumped out of bed and looked out.

What did he see?

He saw a most wonderful sight. Through a little hole in the wall the children had crept in, and they were sitting in the branches of the trees. In every tree that he could see there was a little child. And the trees were so glad to have the children back again that they had covered themselves with blossoms, and were waving their arms gently above the children's heads. The birds were flying about and twittering with delight, and the flowers were looking up through the green grass and laughing. It was a lovely scene, only in one corner it was still winter. It was the farthest corner of the garden, and in it was standing a little boy. He was so small that he could not reach up to the branches of the tree, and he was wandering all round it, crying bitterly. The poor tree was still quite covered with frost and snow, and the North Wind was blowing and roaring above it. "Climb up! little boy," said the Tree, and it bent its branches down as low as it could; but the boy was too tiny.

And the Giant's heart melted as he looked out. "How selfish I have been!" he said; "now I know why the Spring would not come here. I will put that poor little boy on the top of the tree, and then I will knock down the wall, and my garden shall be the children's play-ground for ever and ever." He was really very sorry for what he had done.

So he crept down-stairs and opened the front door quite softly, and went out into the garden. But when the children saw him they were so frightened that they all ran away, and the garden became winter again. Only the little boy did not run, for his eyes were so full of tears that he did not see the Giant coming. And the Giant strode up behind him and took him gently in his hand, and put him up into the tree. And the tree broke at once into blossom, and the birds came and sang on it, and the little boy stretched out his two arms and flung them round the Giant's neck, and kissed him. And the other children, when they saw that the Giant was not wicked any longer, came running back, and with them came the Spring. "It is your garden now, little children," said the Giant, and he took a great axe and knocked down the wall. And when the people were going to market at twelve o'clock they found the Giant playing with the children in the most beautiful garden they had ever seen.

All day long they played, and in the evening they came to the Giant to

bid him good-bye.

"But where is your little companion?" he said, "the boy I put into the tree." The Giant loved him the best because he had kissed him.

"We don't know," answered the children, "he has gone away."

"You must tell him to be sure and come here to-morrow," said the Giant. But the children said that they did not know where he lived, and had never seen him before; and the Giant felt very sad.

Every afternoon, when school was over, the children came and played with the Giant. But the little boy whom the Giant loved was never seen again. The Giant was very kind to all the children, yet he longed for his first little friend, and often spoke of him. "How I would like to see him!" he used to say.

Years went over, and the Giant grew very old and feeble. He could not play about any more, so he sat in a huge armchair, and watched the children at their games, and admired his garden. "I have many beautiful flowers," he said; "but the children are the most beautiful flowers of all."

One winter morning he looked out of his window as he was dressing. He did not hate the Winter now, for he knew that it was merely Spring asleep, and that the flowers were resting.

Suddenly he rubbed his eyes in wonder, and looked and looked. It certainly was a marvelous sight. In the farthest corner of the garden was a tree quite covered with lovely white blossoms. Its branches were all golden, and silver fruit hung down from them, and underneath it stood the little boy he had loved.

Down-stairs ran the Giant in great joy, and out into the garden. He hastened across, and came near to the child. And when he came quite close his face grew red with anger, and he said, "Who hath dared to wound thee?" For on the palms of the child's hands were the prints of two nails, and the prints of two nails were on the little feet.

"Who hath dared to wound thee?" cried the Giant; "tell me, that I may take my big sword and slay him."

"Nay!" answered the child; "but these are the wounds of Love."

"Who art thou?" said the Giant, and a strange awe fell on him, and he knelt before the little child.

And the child smiled on the Giant, and said to him, "You let me play once in your garden; to-day you shall come with me to my garden, which is

Paradise."

And when the children ran in that afternoon, they found the Giant lying dead under the tree, all covered with white blossoms.

THE BLUE PARROT

In a part of Arabia where groves of palms and sweet-scented flowers give the traveller rest after toilsome journeys under burning skies, there reigned a young king whose name was Lino. He had grown up under the wise rule of his father, who had lately died, and though he was only nineteen, he did not believe, like many young men, that he must change all the laws in order to show how clever he was, but was content with the old ones which had made the people happy and the country prosperous. There was only one fault that his subjects had to find with him; and that was that he did not seem in any hurry to be married, in spite of the prayers that they frequently offered him.

The neighbouring kingdom was governed by the Swan fairy, who had an only daughter, the Princess Hermosa, who was as charming in her way as Lino in his. The Swan fairy always had an ambassador at the young king's court, and on hearing the grumbles of the citizens that Lino showed no signs of taking a wife, the good man resolved that *he* would try his hand at matchmaking. "For," he said, "if there is anyone living who is worthy of the Princess Hermosa, he is to be found here. At any rate, I can but try and bring them together."

Now, of course, it was not proper to offer the princess in marriage, and the difficulty was to work upon the unconscious king so as to get the proposal to come from *him*. But the ambassador was well used to the ways of courts, and after several conversations on the art of painting, which Lino loved, he led the talk to portraits, and mentioned carelessly that a particularly fine picture had lately been made of his own princess. "Though, as for a likeness," he concluded, "perhaps it is hardly as good as this small miniature, which was painted a year ago."

The king took it, and looked at it closely.

"Ah!" he sighed, "that must be flattered! It cannot be possible that any woman should be such a miracle of beauty."

"If you could only see her." answered the ambassador.

The king did not reply, but the ambassador was not at all surprised when, the following morning, he was sent for into the royal presence.

"Since you showed me that picture," began Lino, almost before the door was shut, "I have not been able to banish the face of the princess from my thoughts. I have summoned you here to inform you that I am about to send special envoys to the court of the Swan fairy, asking her daughter in marriage."

"I cannot, as you will understand, speak for my mistress in so important a matter," replied the ambassador, stroking his beard in order to conceal the satisfaction he felt. "But I know that she will certainly be highly gratified at your proposal."

"If that is so," cried the king, his whole face beaming with joy, "then, instead of sending envoys, I will go myself, and take you with me. In three days my preparations will be made, and we will set out."

Unluckily for Lino, he had for his neighbour on the other side a powerful magician named Ismenor, who was king of the Isle of Lions, and the father of a hideous daughter, whom he thought the most beautiful creature that ever existed. Riquette, for such was her name, had also fallen in love with a portrait; but it was of King Lino, and she implored her father to give him to her for a husband. Ismenor, who considered that no man lived who was worthy of his treasure, was about to send his chief minister to King Lino on this mission, when the news reached him that the king had already started for the court of the Swan fairy. Riquette was thrown into transports of grief, and implored her father to prevent the marriage, which Ismenor promised to do; and calling for an ugly and humpbacked little dwarf named Rabot, he performed some spells which transported them quickly to a rocky valley through which the king and his escort were bound to pass. When the tramp of horses was heard, the magician took out an enchanted handkerchief, which rendered invisible anyone who touched it. Giving one end to Rabot, and holding the other himself, they walked unseen amongst the horsemen, but not a trace of Lino was to be found. And this was natural enough, because the king, tired out with the excitement and fatigue of the last few days, had bidden the heavy coaches, laden with presents for the princess, to go forwards, while he rested under the palms with a few of his friends. Here Ismenor beheld them, all sound asleep; and casting a spell which prevented their waking till he wished them to did so, he stripped the king of all his clothes and dressed him in those of Rabot, whom he touched with his ring, saying:

"Take the shape of Lino until you have wedded the daughter of the Swan fairy."

And so great was the magician's power that Rabot positively believed himself to be really the king !

When the groom had mounted Lino's horse, and had ridden out of sight, Ismenor aroused the king, who stared with astonishment at the dirty garments in which he was dressed; but before he had time to look about him, the magician caught him up in a cloud, and carried him off to his daughter.

Meantime Rabot had come up with the others, who never guessed for a moment that he was not their own master.

"I am hungry," said he, "give me something to eat at once."

"May it please your majesty," answered the steward, "the tents are not even set up, and it will be at least an hour before your supper is served! We thought — "

"Who taught you to think?" interrupted the false king rudely. "You are nothing but a fool! Get me some horse's flesh directly — it is the best meat in the world!"

The steward could hardly believe his ears. King Lino, the most polite man under the sun, to speak to his faithful servant in such a manner! And to want horse's flesh too! Why, he was so delicate in his appetite that he lived mostly on fruit and cakes. Well, well, there was no knowing what people would come to; and, anyhow, he must obey at once, if he wished to keep his head on his shoulders. Perhaps, after all, it was love which had driven him mad, and, if so by-and-by he might come right again.

Whatever excuses his old servants might invent for their master, by the time the procession reached the Swan fairy's capital there were no more horses left, and they were forced to walk up to the palace on foot. Hiding their surprise as best they could, they begged the king to follow them, dismounting from their own horses, as he, they supposed, preferred to walk. They soon perceived the Swan fairy and her daughter awaiting them on a low balcony, under which the king stopped.

"Madam," he said, "you may be surprised that I have come to ask your daughter's hand in so unceremonious a fashion; but the journey is long, and I was hungry and ate my horse, which is the best meat in the world; and I forced my courtiers to eat theirs also. But for all that I am a great king, and wish to be your son-in-law. And now that is settled, where is Hermosa?"

"Sire," answered the queen, not a little displeased as well as amazed at the king's manner, which was so different from anything she had been led to expect. "You possess my daughter's portrait, and it can have made but little impression on you if you don't recognise her at once."

"I don't remember any portrait," replied Rabot; "but perhaps it may be in my pocket after all." And he searched everywhere, while the ladies-in-waiting looked on with astonishment, but of course found nothing. When he had finished he turned to the princess, who stood there blushing and angry, and said:

"If it is you whom I have come to marry, I think you are very beautiful, and I am sure if I had even seen your portrait I should have remembered it. Let us have the wedding as soon as possible; and, meantime, I should like to go to sleep, for your country is very different from mine, and I can assure you that after walking over stones and sand for days and days one needs a little rest."

And without waiting for a reply he bade one of the pages conduct him to his room, where he was soon snoring so loud that he could be heard at the other end of the town.

As soon as he was out of their sight, the poor princess flung herself into her mother's arms, and burst into tears. For fifteen days she had had King Lino's portrait constantly before her, while the letter from their own ambassador speaking of the young man's grace and charm had never left her pocket. True, the portrait was faithful enough, but how could that fair outside contain so rough and rude a soul? Yet this even she might have forgiven had the king shown any of the signs of love and admiration to which she had been so long accustomed. As for her mother, the poor Swan fairy was so bewildered at the extraordinary manners of her new son-in-law, that she was almost speechless.

Matters were in this state when King Lino's chamberlain begged for a private audience of her majesty, and no sooner were they alone than he told her that he feared that his master had suddenly gone mad, or had fallen under the spell of some magician.

"I had been lost in astonishment before," said he, "but now that he has failed to recognise the princess, and no longer possesses her portrait, which he never would part from for a single instant, my amazement knows no bounds. Perhaps, madam, your fairy gifts may be able to discover the reason of this change in one whose courtesy was the talk of the kingdom." And with a low bow he took his departure.

The queen stood where the chamberlain left her, thinking deeply. Suddenly her face cleared, and going to an old chest which she kept in a secret room, she drew from it a small mirror. In this mirror she could see faithfully reflected whatever she wished, and at this moment she desired above all things to behold King Lino *as he really was.*

Ah! the chamberlain was right! It was not he who was lying on his bed snoring till the whole palace shook beneath him. No, *this* was her real son-in-law — the man dressed in dirty clothes, and imprisoned in one of Ismenor's strongest towers, and kissing the portrait of Hermosa, which had escaped the wizard's notice, owing to the young king having worn it, for better concealment, tied amongst his hair. Calling hastily to her daughter, she bade her also look, and Hermosa had the pleasure of gazing on Lino, who was behaving exactly as she could have wished. The mirror was still in her hand when the door of the prison opened, and there entered the hideous Riquette, who, from her upraised eyes, seemed to be begging from Lino some favour which he refused to grant. Of course Hermosa and her mother could not hear their words, but from Riquette's angry face as she left the room, it was not difficult to guess what had happened. But the mirror had more to tell, for it appeared that in fury at her rejection by the king, Riquette had ordered four strong men to scourge him till he fainted, which was done in the sight of Hermosa, who in horror dropped the mirror, and would have fallen, had she not been caught by her mother.

"Control yourself, my child," said the fairy. "We have need of all our wits if we are to rescue the king from the power of those wicked people. And

first it is necessary to know who the man that has taken his name and his face really is."

Then, picking up the mirror, she wished that she might behold the false lover; and the glass gave back a vision of a dirty, greasy groom, lying, dressed as he was, on her bed of state.

"So this is the trick Ismenor hoped to play us! Well, we will have our revenge, whatever it costs us to get it. Only we must be very careful not to let him guess that he has not deceived us, for his skill in magic is greater than mine, and I shall have to be very prudent. To begin with, I must leave you, and if the false king asks why, then answer that I have to settle some affairs on the borders of my kingdom. Meanwhile, be sure you treat him most politely, and arrange fêtes to amuse him. If he shows any sign of being suspicious, you can even give him to understand that, on your marriage, I intend to give up the crown to your husband. And now farewell!" So saying, the Swan fairy waved her hand, and a cloud came down and concealed her, and nobody imagined that the beautiful white cloud that was blown so rapidly across the sky was the chariot that was carrying the Swan fairy to the tower of Ismenor.

Now the tower was situated in the midst of a forest, so the queen thought that, under cover of the dark trees, it would be quite easy for her to drop to earth unseen. But the tower was so thoroughly enchanted that the more she tried to reach the ground the tighter something tried to hold her back. At length, by putting forth all the power she possessed, she managed to descend to the foot of the tower, and there, weak and faint as she was with her exertions, she lost no time in working her spells, and found that she could only overcome Ismenor by means of a stone from the ring of Gyges. But how was she to get this ring? For the magic book told her that Ismenor guarded it night and day among his most precious treasures. However, get it she must, and in the meantime the first step was to see the royal prisoner himself. So, drawing out her tablets, she wrote as follows:

"The bird which brings you this letter is the Swan fairy, mother of Hermosa, who loves you as much as you love her!" And after this assurance, she related the wicked plot of which he had been the victim. Then, quickly changing herself into a swallow, she began to fly round the tower, till she discovered the window of Lino's prison. It was so high up that bars seemed needless, especially as four soldiers were stationed in the passage outside, therefore the fairy was able to enter, and even to hop on his shoulder, but he was so much occupied with gazing at the princess's portrait that it was some time before she could attract his attention. At last she gently scratched his cheek with the corner of the note, and he looked round with a start. On perceiving the swallow he knew at once that help had come, and tearing open the letter, he wept with joy on seeing the words it contained, and asked a thousand questions as to Hermosa, which the swallow was unable to answer, though, by repeated nods, she signed to him to read further. "Must I indeed pretend to wish to marry that horrible Riquette?" he cried, when he had finished. "Can I obtain the stone from the magician?"

Accordingly the next morning, when Riquette paid him her daily visit, he received her much more graciously than usual. The magician's daughter could not contain her delight at this change, and in answer to her expressions of joy, Lino told her that he had had a dream by which he had learned the inconstancy of Hermosa; also that a fairy had appeared and informed him that if he wished to break the bonds which bound him to the faithless princess and transfer his affections to the daughter of Ismenor, he must have in his possession for a day and a night a stone from the ring of Gyges, now in the possession of the magician. This news so enchanted Riquette, that she flung her arms round the king's neck and embraced him tenderly, greatly to his disgust, as he would infinitely have preferred the sticks of the soldiers. However, there was no help for it, and he did his best to seem pleased, till Riquette relieved him by announcing that she must lose no time in asking her father and obtaining from him the precious stone.

His daughter's request came as a great surprise to Ismenor, whose suspicions were instantly excited; but, think as he would, he could not see any means by which the king, so closely guarded, might have held communication with the Swan fairy. Still, he would do nothing hastily, and, hiding his dismay, he told Riquette that his only wish was to make her happy, and that as she wished so much for the stone he would fetch it for her. Then he went into the closet where all his spells were worked, and in a short time he discovered that his enemy the Swan fairy was at that moment inside his palace.

"So that is it!" he said, smiling grimly. "Well, she shall have a stone by all means, but a stone that will turn everyone who touches it into marble." And placing a small ruby in a box, he returned to his daughter.

"Here is the talisman which will gain you the love of King Lino," he said; "but be sure you give him the box unopened, or else the stone will lose all its virtue." With a cry of joy Riquette snatched the box from his hands, and ran off to the prison, followed by her father, who, holding tightly the enchanted handkerchief, was able, unseen, to watch the working of the spell. As he expected, at the foot of the tower stood the Swan fairy, who had had the imprudence to appear in her natural shape, waiting for the stone which the prince was to throw to her. Eagerly she caught the box as it fell from the prince's hands, but no sooner had her fingers touched the ruby, than a curious hardening came over her, her limbs stiffened, and her tongue could hardly utter the words "We are betrayed."

"Yes, you *are* betrayed," cried Ismenor, in a terrible voice; "and *you*," he continued, dragging the king to the window, "you shall turn into a parrot, and a parrot you will remain until you can persuade Hermosa to crush in your head."

He had hardly finished before a blue parrot flew out into the forest; and the magician, mounting in his winged chariot, set off for the Isle of Swans, where he changed everybody into statues, exactly in the positions in which he found them, not even excepting Rabot himself. Only Hermosa was spared, and her he ordered to get into his chariot beside him. In a few minutes he reached the Forest of Wonders, when the magician got down, and dragged the unhappy princess out after him.

"I have changed your mother into a stone, and your lover into a parrot," said he, "and you are to become a tree, and a tree you will remain until you have crushed the head of the person you love best in the world. But I will leave you your mind and memory, that your tortures may be increased a thousand-fold."

Great magician as he was, Ismenor could not have invented a more terrible fate had he tried for a hundred years. The hours passed wearily by for the poor princess, who longed for a wood-cutter's axe to put an end to her misery. How were they to be delivered from their doom? And even supposing that King Lino *did* fly that way, there were thousands of blue parrots in the forest, and how was she to know him, or he her? As to her mother — ah! that was too bad to think about! So, being a woman, she kept on thinking.

Meanwhile the blue parrot flew about the world, making friends wherever he went, till, one day, he entered the castle of an old wizard who had just married a beautiful young wife. Grenadine, for such was her name, led a very dull life, and was delighted to have a playfellow, so she gave him a golden cage to sleep in, and delicious fruits to eat. Only in one way did he disappoint her — he never would talk as other parrots did.

"If you only knew how happy it would make me, I'm sure you would try," she was fond of saying; but the parrot did not seem to hear her.

One morning, however, she left the room to gather some flowers, and the parrot, finding himself alone, hopped to the table, and, picking up a pencil, wrote some verses on a piece of paper. He had just finished when he was startled by a noise, and letting fall the pencil, he flew out of the window.

Now hardly had he dropped the pencil when the wizard lifted a corner of the curtain which hung over the doorway, and advanced into the room. Seeing a paper on the table, he picked it up, and great was his surprise as he read:

Fair princess, to win your grace,
I will hold discourse with you;
Silence, though, were more in place
than chattering like a cockatoo.

"I half suspected it was enchanted," murmured the wizard to himself. And he fetched his books and searched them, and found that instead of being a parrot, the bird was really a king who had fallen under the wrath of a magician, and that magician the man whom the wizard hated most in the world. Eagerly he read on, seeking for some means of breaking the enchantment, and at last, to his great joy, he discovered the remedy. Then he hurried to his wife, who was lying on some cushions under the tree on which the parrot had perched, and informed her that her favourite was really the king of a great country, and that, if she would whistle for the bird, they would all go together to a certain spot in the Forest of Marvels, "where I will restore him to his own shape. Only you must not be afraid or cry out, whatever I do," added he, "or everything will be spoilt." The wizard's wife jumped up in an instant, so delighted was she, and began to whistle the song that the parrot loved; but as he did not wish it to be known that he had been listening to the conversation he waited until she had turned her back, when he flew down from the tree and alighted on her shoulder. Then they got

into a golden boat, which carried them to a clearing in the forest, where three tall trees stood by themselves.

"I want these trees for my magic fire," he said to his wife; "put the parrot on that branch, he will be quite safe, and go yourself to a little distance. If you stay too near, you may get your head crushed in their fall."

At these words, the parrot suddenly remembered the prophecy of Ismenor, and held himself ready, his heart beating at the thought that in one of those trees he beheld Hermosa. Meanwhile, the magician took a spade, and loosened the earth of the roots of the three trees so that they might all fall together. Directly the parrot observed them totter he spread his wings and flew right under the middle one, which was the most beautiful of the three. There was a crash, then Lino and Hermosa stood facing each other, clasped hand in hand.

After the first few moments, the princess's thoughts turned to her mother, and falling at the feet of the magician, who was smiling with delight at the success of his plan, she implored him to help them once more, and to give the Swan fairy back her proper shape.

"That is not so easy," said he, "but I will try what I can do." And transporting himself to his palace to obtain a little bottle of poisoned water, he waited till nightfall, and started at once for Ismenor's tower. Of course, had Ismenor consulted his books, he would have seen what his enemy was doing, he might have protected himself; but he had been eating and drinking too much, and had gone to bed, sleeping heavily. Changing himself into a bat, the magician flew into the room, and hiding himself in the curtains, he poured all the liquid over Ismenor's face, so that he died without a groan. At the same instant, the Swan fairy became a woman again, for no magician, however powerful, can work spells which last beyond his own life.

So when the Swan fairy returned to her capital she found all her courtiers waiting at the gate to receive her, and in their midst, beaming with happiness, Hermosa and King Lino. Standing behind them, though a long way off, was Rabot; but his dirty clothes had given place to clean ones, when his earnest desire was granted, and the princess had made him head of her stables.

And here we must bid them all farewell, feeling sure they will have many years of happiness before them after the terrible trials through which they have passed.

THE HIPPOGRIFF AND THE DRAGON

ot long ago there lived in a cave full of dark holes and ugly shadows an old and feeble Dragon, who had nobody in the world to take care of him. He was the last of that tribe which once waged terrible war upon mankind, and all his relations and friends had been killed off by this same race of men, who declared that, unless they did take such measures, the dragons would not only kill them and their wives and children, but eat them into the bargain. Perhaps this was true, for the dragons had never been accustomed to eat anything but meat, and so they felt actually obliged to supply themselves, two or three times a week, with a plump boy or girl or a well-seasoned old lady.

But all those exciting days were passed; now the last Dragon had just strength enough to crawl slowly about, setting snares to catch birds and rabbits for his dinner. So feeble was he that you could scarcely have terrified him more than by inviting him to attack a human being. He was very lonely and unhappy, and would have been far more so except that in a cave nearby dwelt a Hippogriff who was in exactly the same circumstances, alone, almost helpless, and the last of his race. The dragons and hippogriffs had once been deadly enemies, and two of the animals meeting in a forest path would have torn each other in pieces without stopping to say "Good-morning"; but this pair had suffered so many hardships that they were only too glad to forget old grievances and become intimate friends.

One morning the Dragon rose early, after a miserable night, and when he had breakfasted on a cold crow's wing, left from yesterday's dinner, he took his cane, and crawled out into the sunshine, hoping to see the Hippogriff. Sure enough, there sat his friend, also sunning himself, at the door of his own cave.

"Well," said the Dragon, "what sort of a night have you had?"

"Bad, bad!" groaned the Hippogriff. "The fact is, I was too hungry to sleep. We can't stand this much longer. A good half-ox or a tender young calf would set us both up; but we are too weak to provide for ourselves. Our days are numbered."

"I've been thinking it over in the watches of the night," said the Dragon, "and I've come to the conclusion that we'd better go to the nearest village and see if we can't get employment, and so be able to start a little account at the butcher's. I think I could carry stones or bite down trees as soon as I get my strength up; and I know you could sweep out rooms with your tail."

"There's only one trouble," said the Hippogriff thoughtfully. "As soon as the people saw us coming, they would set upon us and kill us before listening to a word."

"Men are not what they once were," said the Dragon, shaking his head wisely. "They talk a great deal more than the knights we used to know, and they do a great deal less. Get your stick, my friend, and let us start while we still have strength to crawl along. Trust me, it's the only thing to do."

The Hippogriff was a little doubtful, but he had the greatest confidence in his friend. The Dragon always believed so firmly in himself that the Hippogriff thought he must have good grounds for doing so, and it would be very silly not to believe in him, too. So he went in for his stick, gave a farewell look at his cave, and then, taking the Dragon's arm, set off down the hill that led to the village.

"Shall we ever see our homes again?" he murmured, in a sad voice, after the first half mile. "Alas! I am afraid not."

"Who cares if we don't," said the Dragon, "if we get other homes ten times as good?"

And as that seemed reasonable, the Hippogriff said meekly, "You are quite right," and went stumbling along without further complaint.

All the forenoon long they journeyed; and though faint and hungry, they dared not stop, for fear their strength would desert them utterly. The

steeple of the village church seemed hardly nearer than in the morning, and not a soul did they meet or pass upon the way.

"I could eat a caterpillar with relish," said the Hippogriff, at length. "O brother, think of the good old days when we should have scorned a caterpillar, except for dessert, after a hearty meal of a knight and his horse."

"I don't think of the good old days," answered the Dragon, still undaunted, though he could scarcely limp along. "I have fixed my mind on the good time coming, and there I mean it shall stay."

They staggered on until two o'clock in the afternoon; and then, just as they were about to lie down by the roadside in utter despair, the Dragon caught sight of something which put new courage into his failing limbs.

"Stop!" he whispered, grasping the Hippogriff's arm. "Look over in that field, and tell me what you see."

The Hippogriff looked.

"It's a maiden," he answered, "sitting under a tree, holding in her hand one of those queer things they call books."

"We must go over there and talk with her," said the Dragon. "No doubt she can tell us something about the village people, and we will send her on in advance to announce our intentions. But we must circle about, so as to approach her from the back. If she sees us coming, she will be terribly frightened, and run, and we couldn't possibly overtake her."

They climbed the fence, and began cautiously approaching the young woman, who was really so absorbed in reading a Greek play that there was not the slightest danger of her seeing or hearing anything. Only once was the silence broken; and then the Hippogriff ventured timidly, "*She* wouldn't make a bad dinner!"

"Hush!" said the wise Dragon. "That would do very well for to-day, but what would become of us to-morrow? The village people would turn out in a body, and hunt us down. No! I have become a law-abiding citizen."

Meantime the young lady sat intently reading her book, and sometimes consulting other volumes; and, when the two travelers were within a few feet of her, the Dragon gave a delicate cough. She slowly turned her head and saw them. The Hippogriff, trying to look as gentle as possible, laid one claw on his heart, and made a low bow, while the Dragon gazed at her with a cheerful smile. Still they both expected her to give a blood-curdling shriek and spring to her feet in terror. It was evident that they knew nothing about this particular kind of young woman. She settled her eye-glasses firmly upon her nose, and looked the creatures over.

"Who are you," she asked, in a high, clear tone. "Can you talk?"

This was very confusing to the Dragon and Hippogriff. The thought darted through their minds: "If a mere girl isn't afraid of us, what can we expect from the village authorities?"

"Oh, yes, ma'am," said the Dragon, recovering himself first, "we talk and walk and eat (when we can get anything). We are not in the least different from other folks, though we may look so; and that's why we've made up our minds to move to the village."

"What are your names?"

"I am a Dragon, and my friend here is a Hippogriff."

A look of joy flitted over the young woman's face.

"How very interesting!" she cried, in a tone of such rapture that the Dragon's spirits rose at once. "How wonderful that such an experience should be mine! Come, sit down here on the grass and tell me about yourselves."

The Dragon and the Hippogriff were very glad indeed to sit down, and the former especially was well inclined to talk. He began at the beginning of dragon and hippogriff history, and told all he knew and all he had ever heard about those remarkable creatures and their warfare with men. When he had finished, his listener drew a breath of delight.

"This is amazing!" said she. "I wouldn't have believed it if I hadn't heard it with my own ears."

"But what do you think of our chances of being allowed to live in the village, ma'am?" ventured the Hippogriff.

"They never would permit it in the world," she said, wrinkling her brows in thought. "The very sight of you would frighten them to death."

"But you are not frightened?" suggested the Dragon.

She smiled at him loftily.

"No, but I am an Advanced Young Woman. I have had a college course, and none of the village folk are in the least like me. They would expect you to eat them up."

"But we would promise not to," urged the Hippogriff, who was actually so hungry that he could not speak of food without tears.

But the Advanced Young Woman was thinking so hard that she took no notice of him at all.

"Ah!" cried she at length, in triumph. "I have it! You shall become vegetarians."

"I will become anything that is proper, ma'am," said the Dragon meekly. "What sort of creatures are they? I shouldn't want to give up my tail and my claws."

"You would merely have to give up eating meat, and then of course nobody would be afraid of you. It will be a most interesting experiment. Perhaps we can even modify your teeth, and make you graminivorous."

This ambition was quite beyond the creatures' comprehension; and so they said nothing, but tried to look wise, as people often do who don't understand.

"Just over the brow of this hill," added the Advanced Young Woman, "is a cottage my father built me for a study, so that I might retire there beyond the hearing of the world." (She meant the village.) "Now you shall go there with me, and after dark, I will bring you some supper. You must on no account step outside the door, and to-morrow, immediately after breakfast, I will be with you."

Meanwhile she had packed her books together, and, making them into a nice heavy bundle, started away over the hillside, driving the two creatures before her; and although she was both slight and young, they were really quite afraid of her, and went meekly stumbling along, hand in hand.

"She seems to take a great interest in us," whispered the Hippogriff, when the Advanced Young Woman was occupied in unlocking the door. "She must think us very remarkable."

"Hush," said the Dragon solemnly. "There is more in this than we understand."

And there was!

"There," said the young woman, when she had ushered them into the one large room that occupied the entire floor of the cottage, "now be very quiet and patient. To prevent accidents, I think I'll lock the door on the outside."

And this she did before hastening away.

When she was fairly gone, the Dragon and the Hippogriff looked about them. The room was filled with all sorts of strange articles, which they had never seen or heard of. The walls were lined with books; and on the large table there was an inkstand, an unabridged dictionary, a microscope, a herbarium, an astrolabe, a sextant, and other queer things used by Advanced Young Women, but which I don't in the least understand, any more than the Dragon and the Hippogriff did.

"I don't like this," said the Hippogriff, looking about him.

"Nor I," said the Dragon. "But let's wait until she comes back, and see what will happen."

Presently there was a rattling at the door, and in came their hostess tugging a large pail, and looking much excited.

"I've brought your supper," said she cheerfully. "Oatmeal, far more nutritious than meat!"

She poured the pudding into two large dishes, and placed it on the floor before them, and while they tried to eat it, and smeared their jaws and burned their tongues, she walked round and round, studying them from every point of view.

"Vertebrates!" she exclaimed, adding, as she paused beside the Dragon, "Would it annoy you if I tried to count your vertebrae while you are eating?"

"Not at all," said the miserable Dragon, though he had no idea what his vertebrae were. "I believe I won't take anything more to eat, thank you, ma'am."

Then the Advanced Young Woman was perfectly happy. She pinched their backbones to see how they were made, counted their claws, and examined their teeth; and the horrible-looking animals were by this time so depressed that they never thought of objecting.

"Ah!" murmured she, "what a precious privilege, and how Professor Cervix would envy me!" It was quite dark before she could tear herself away from them. "Now," said she, at last, gathering up the dishes, "take a good night's rest, in order to be perfectly fresh in the morning. Then I intend to sketch you."

When the sound of her footsteps had quite died away, the Hippogriff looked at the Dragon, and gave a hollow groan.

"Are you hungry?" he asked.

"I could eat a buffalo, hide and all," owned the Dragon frankly. "Still if one were here I should try to resist it. If it's possible to become a law-abiding vegetarian, I'm the Dragon to do it."

"I believe myself the stuff she gave us was rank poison," said the melancholy Hippogriff. "I ate very little of it, but I feel extremely queer."

"Wait till it begins to nourish you," said the hopeful Dragon, who felt quite as unsettled as his friend, but had no intention of showing it. "Remember, she told us it was far more nutritious than meat; and if that is true, we shall soon begin to feel it in our legs and claws. Now go to sleep, as I shall, and make the best of it." So saying, he curled his head under his shoulder, folded his claws, and was soon far on the road to Dragon Dreamland.

Next morning the Advanced Young Woman reached the cottage by the time the early birds had begun to charm away the dusk. She brought a steaming kettle of cracked wheat, and this she poured out before the two monsters with so gracious an air that they hadn't the heart to tell her they hated the sight of it. Instead they each made her a polite bow, and tried with all their might to force a little down their unwilling throats.

The young woman, however, never noticed how hard a time of it they had. She was altogether too busy, first in getting her sketching materials together, and then in drawing the outline of her guests from every point of view. She sketched them sitting, standing and lying. She sketched their faces, their claws, their tails. Never, since time began, had there been such an exhaustive study of dragons and hippogriffs. She worked all day long, forgetting to stop for dinner; and the worst of it was, the Hippogriff thought, she forgot their dinner also, and they languished until nightfall without even a dish of oatmeal. However, when she went home, very tired, but with an undaunted resolution still shining on her brow, she left them the cold cracked wheat for supper. That night they did not talk; their terror of the future was too great.

Things went on in this way for a week, the Dragon and the Hippogriff trying to become good vegetarians, and growing weaker every day, and their hostess worrying them almost out of their senses by asking them questions about their previous history, and, as the Hippogriff said, trying to pry into their family affairs. The truth was that she knew this to be a splendid opportunity for studying the habits of animals which most people consider fabulous, and she was determined to make the most of it.

"Now" said she, on leaving them one night, "I hope you'll go to bed early, for I want you to look particularly fresh to-morrow. A dear friend of mine, Professor Cervix, is coming to see you, though he doesn't in the least suspect you are here. I intend to surprise him, and then we shall consult together about donating you to a museum."

"What is a museum?" asked the Hippogriff feebly.

"It is a large collection of animals, shut up in cages," said the Advanced Young Woman, with cheerfulness. "Good-night. Don't give yourselves any uneasiness. Whatever we decide upon, you need take no responsibility. I will arrange everything."

And the worst of it was, they knew she would. For a long time after she was gone, they said nothing at all; but at last the Hippogriff remarked solemnly: "A hundred years ago or more, the fairies danced one night on the green, and we hippogriffs lay in the woods and watched them. They were practicing the Vanishing Charm."

"I remember," said the Dragon, "we dragons were there, too, in the opposite wood. We meant to fall upon you, and eat you up, when the fairies were gone; but we got so interested in their Vanishing Charm that we forgot all about it. Do you remember what they sang?"

"Perfectly," said the Hippogriff. "Shall we try it?"

"Yes. I don't know where we should be after we had vanished; but nothing could be worse than this. Come, let's begin. It may take a long time."

So they sat down in the middle of the room, clasped claws in the Vanishing Grip, and began a solemn chant:—

Criss-cross,
Gain is loss.
The gold in the earth is nothing but dross.
Heigh ho!
Who can know
But the elves where the flowers of elf-land blow!

"My tail is gone!" said the Dragon, in an excited whisper.
"So's my left ear!" cried the Hippogriff. "Come, faster!"

If you double under as I double over,
Then lightning is thunder and redtop is clover.
So turn it about, now slow and now fast,
Till the end is beginning, and middle is last.

"There go my claws!" cried the Hippogriff.

"And my hind legs!" said the Dragon. "Oh, how comfortable I am! I haven't felt so light since I was a baby."

They chanted faster and faster: they were wild with joy. When the Hippogriff felt his backbone going, he gave an exultant shout to think the Advanced Young Woman would never count his vertebrae again. But that was his last thought in this world. The song was finished, the cottage was silent; the Hippogriff and Dragon had vanished.

Next morning the Advanced Young Woman went early to her retreat, that she might be sure the two animals were prepared for meeting the learned Professor Cervix. She opened the door and looked in. Not a trace of living creature was to be seen. Even her precious drawings had disappeared: for the Dragon had laid one claw on them as he chanted the vanishing words, and they also had felt the charm. But the Advanced Young Woman, though she was disappointed, felt no surprise.

"Of course there's no such thing," said she. "They're nothing but fabulous monsters. I must have dreamed them."

But at that very moment the Dragon and the Hippogriff, young and strong, and no larger than butterflies, were telling their adventures to the elf queen, who laughed over them until her poppy throne swayed in the breeze.

"Trouble yourselves no further about food and shelter," said she, when they had finished. "For those that live in this Vanished Land need no roof to cover them, and honey dew is all their food."

THE WILLOW TREE

There was not a prettier girl in Hing-Shan than Li-Ho, the only daughter of a rich old mandarin, who lived in a beautiful house, two stories in height, which is a rare thing in China, and showed that the owner was a man of great wealth.

Besides being a very pretty girl, Li-Ho was always dressed in the brightest, softest and most expensive silks that her father could buy.

She liked best to wear peach-colored silk, embroidered with silver, and if you could have seen her sitting on her balcony, on a moonlight night, with flowers twined in her hair, and the shining peach-colored silk falling in soft folds about her, you would have thought her the prettiest girl you had ever seen, and worthy to marry a prince.

But Li-Ho did not care for princes. In fact she did not think of them at all, for she had fallen in love with her father's secretary, whose name was Wang. He lived in the gardener's cottage on an island in the river which ran through the garden. The old mandarin, whose name was Hing-Fung, did not like the state of affairs at all, and had forbidden the young man to come near the house, at the same time forbidding Li-Ho to leave it, so that the lovers might have no chance of meeting. He went still further, for he betrothed Li-Ho to an old Ta-jin or Duke who was very rich.

One night Hing-Fung came to his daughter as she was sitting on her balcony and told her that he had made all the arrangements for her marriage to the Ta-jin.

"I don't love him," sobbed Li-Ho. "I love Wang, and I cannot marry any one else."

"Put Wang out of your mind," replied her father, sternly. "Wang shall never be your husband. I have promised the Ta-jin that you shall marry him when the peach tree blossoms."

Now the willow tree was in blossom then, for it was early in the year, but the peach tree would not bloom until the spring.

So from that day Li-Ho watched the unfolding of the buds of the peach tree which grew close to her window, with sorrow and dread in her heart.

"Is it possible that Wang is dead?" she wondered, "or has he forgotten all about me?"

Wang was very unhappy, too. He was not dead, neither had he forgotten Li-Ho. He thought of her day and night, and at last, one evening, he sent her a message.

Li-Ho was sitting on her balcony as usual, when a little boat made out of half a cocoa-nut shell, and fitted with a tiny sail, floated right to her feet.

She ran to pick it up, and inside it she found a colored bead she had given her lover, which was a sure proof the boat came from Wang; and also a piece of bamboo paper, on which these words were written:

When the willow fades away,
And the peach tree groweth gay,
Tell me, sweetheart, can it be
They will steal my love from me?

It was sweet and romantic to have a message from her lover come in this way, and it made Li-Ho very happy. So she took her ivory tablets from the bosom of her peach-colored dress, and wrote on them:

When the peach tree blooms, sweetheart,
Thou and I must weep and part.
Hasten, then, to take the prize
Ere 'tis seen by robber's eyes.

Li-Ho knew that her lover would understand this kind of language, so she put the tablets in the boat and lighted a stick of frankincense and placed it on the bow.

Then she leaned over the balcony and watched the little boat sail away in the darkness, saying softly to herself, "He will come for me before my wedding day."

But Li-Ho was not so sure after all, for through the still night air, heavy with the scent of flowers, she half imagined she could hear the blossoms on the willow tree sighing faintly:

"It will be too late; we are dying!" For Wang had promised, the last time they met, that he would come for her while the willow was still in blossom.

And then the buds on the peach tree seemed to say:

"We are nearly ready to open. Then she will marry the Ta-jin."

Wang waited for the return of the frail little boat, but the waves brought it to his feet at last; and when he read the verse on Li-Ho's ivory tablets, his smile went up to the corner of his eyes, as Chinese smiles generally do.

Then he went into the cottage and called the gardener and his wife. "Do you know when the Ta-jin is coming?" he asked.

"Indeed, I do," replied the gardener. "The betrothal feast is set for next Thursday, for the moon will then be lucky.

"The mandarin has ordered the gardeners to take six dozen carp out of the fish ponds, and there are to be golden and silver pheasants on the table."

"And as many oysters as his guests can eat," chimed in his wife. "And six casks of wine to be broached."

"I hear that such a casket of jewels as the Ta-jin is bringing his bride, has never been seen before," continued the gardener. "There is a necklace of pearls, and each pearl is as big as a sparrow's egg — "

"Oh, how stupid you are!" interrupted his wife. "As big as a pigeon's egg, you mean."

"I said sparrow's egg, imbecile!" retorted the gardener.

"Idiot!" repeated the woman, angrily. "I say pigeon's egg!"

"Never mind," Wang broke in. "It doesn't matter which. What I want to know is, whether you can borrow me one of the servant's dresses, and smuggle me into the banquet room that night."

Now, both the gardener and his wife knew about Wang's love story, but neither of them dared to help him. They were afraid to risk the anger of such a rich and powerful mandarin as Li-Ho's father.

What preparations there were for the betrothal feast! Hing-Fung never stopped giving orders from morning till night. Servants were running hither and thither all the time; the banquet hall was swept, and strewn with sweet-scented leaves, and the walls and roof hung with colored silk lanterns and fans.

Li-Ho was the only one that was not happy and busy. She would sit on her balcony, with her embroidery lying idle on her lap, as she gazed wistfully across the river which separated her from her lover.

Then the morning of the betrothal feast came. The peach tree was covered with lovely pink blossoms, while the willow blossoms hung, faded and drooping on the tree.

Li-Ho could not stay on the balcony when she saw this, so she went into her room and sat on a couch, with her head resting on her hand, watching her attendants as they spread out on the floor the beautiful silk dresses the Ta-jin had sent as a present to his bride.

But Li-Ho was sad, and cared nothing for these at all, although they were in all the colors of the rainbow, pale blue, and pink, and yellow, and purple, embroidered in gold and silver.

One of them was of peach-colored silk, embroidered with pearls, and the woman said, "This is just the dress for a bride." But Li-Ho shook her head. "I will not wear peach-color any more," she said.

Neither was she interested when they brought her the casket of jewels which the Ta-jin had sent by his servants, and of which the gardener and his wife had spoken. There were diamonds and rubies of a size fit to be worn by the Emperor himself; and the necklace of pearls went twice around Li-Ho's neck and hung down nearly to her waist.

At last the time came when she must be dressed for her betrothal, and her attendants selected a beautiful blue silk dress, embroidered all over with golden butterflies; because in China butterflies are looked upon as a symbol of married happiness.

Then they fastened the pearls around her throat, and put some shining jewels in her hair. "This is going to be a great lady," they said. "Flowers in the hair were only for common people."

When they had finished dressing her, Li-Ho sent them all away. She was tired with their talk about the Ta-jin, and she wanted to go out on the balcony once more and see if the willow blossoms were quite faded, and if there was no last message from Wang coming to her on the water.

Pretty soon one of the women came back to say that one of the servants wished to speak to her. "Let him come in," said Li-Ho, impatiently.

Then a young man entered wearing a long blue cotton robe and a

broad straw hat which half concealed his face. As soon as they were alone he took off his hat, making Li-Ho a low sweeping bow, and there was Wang himself!

For a moment she could not believe it, but when he took her in his arms and kissed her, crumpling up all the golden butterflies in his eagerness, she knew it was really her lover, who had come to save her from marrying the Ta-jin.

"Oh, Wang! how did you get here?" she cried, and Wang told her he came disguised as a beggar. "But when I came to the door of the banquet room to ask for alms, every one was too busy to listen to me. So I managed to slip behind a screen, and afterwards find my way to your room."

"But how did you get this dress?" asked Li-Ho, touching it.

"I found it behind the screen where one of the servants must have left it," Wang replied. "And now, Li-Ho, how can I disguise you? We must pass behind the screen, and through the banquet room into the garden, and across the bridge to the gardener's cottage."

Li-Ho's old nurse had left one of her old garments in the room and it covered up all of Li-Ho's bridal finery except her pretty little gold-embroidered shoes. "Never mind my shoes," she said, "I shall run so fast no one will see them."

Then she took her distaff in her hand, because she did not want to be an idle, useless wife to Wang, and she gave him the box of jewels to carry. Probably they should not have taken the jewels, although the Ta-jin had given them to Li-Ho, and it might have been that Wang was in too great a hurry to ask what was in the box.

"Come, my darling," said Wang. "The willow blossoms droop upon the bough, we must delay no longer!" And, indeed, as the lovers crept behind the screen, a light breeze shook the last blossoms of the willow to the ground.

"Oh, if my father should see us," whispered Li-Ho, holding her lover's hand very tightly.

"You need not be afraid," said Wang. "I have prayed to the good Genii not to let him catch us. If he comes too near, they will change us into two stars or perhaps two turtle-doves. You would not mind that, would you?"

"No indeed, I do not mind anything but parting from you," replied Li-Ho. Then they crossed the garden and Wang led his sweetheart towards the bridge.

They could have run faster had it not been for Li-Ho's pretty little shoes; so they had only reached the foot of the bridge when Hing-Fung came rushing after them with a whip in his hand.

"Stop the thief who has stolen my daughter," he cried furiously. "Stop! Stop!"

But Wang did not stop at all. He put Li-Ho in front of him and she ran across the bridge first, with her distaff, while he followed her with the casket of jewels. Behind them came the mandarin brandishing his whip.

Now, the good Genii saw that the mandarin was gaining on the lovers, and that they had no chance to escape. "What shall we do?" said one to the other. "They will flog Wang to death and shut up Li-Ho for the rest of her life."

"Let us change them into two turtle-doves," said one Geni. "Then they may be happy after all."

So just as the mandarin put out his hand to seize Wang by the shoulder, splash! the box of jewels fell into the water and Wang and Li-Ho were changed into two beautiful doves, which flew away at once out of the mandarin's reach, leaving the mandarin there with the whip in his hand, and the Ta-jin's jewels at the bottom of the river.

Wang and Li-Ho built a cosy nest in the garden from which they could watch the willow and the peach tree bloom and fade without any fear of being parted from each other.

What became of the mandarin, I do not know, but I have an idea that he had a rather unpleasant time explaining to the Ta-jin how all these things happened.

THE PARADISE OF CHILDREN

ong, long ago, when this old world was in its tender infancy, there was a child, named Epimetheus, who never had either father or mother; and, that he might not be lonely, another child, fatherless and motherless like himself, was sent from a far country, to live with him, and be his playfellow and helpmate. Her name was Pandora.

The first thing that Pandora saw, when she entered the cottage where Epimetheus dwelt, was a great box. And almost the first question which she put to him, after crossing the threshold, was this, —

"Epimetheus, what have you in that box?"

"My dear little Pandora," answered Epimetheus, "that is a secret, and you must be kind enough not to ask any questions about it. The box was left here to be kept safely, and I do not myself know what it contains."

"But who gave it to you?" asked Pandora. "And where did it come from?"

"That is a secret, too," replied Epimetheus.

"How provoking!" exclaimed Pandora, pouting her lip. "I wish the great ugly box were out of the way!"

"Oh come, don't think of it any more," cried Epimetheus. "Let us run out of doors, and have some nice play with the other children."

It is thousands of years since Epimetheus and Pandora were alive; and the world, nowadays, is a very different sort of thing from what it was in their time. Then, everybody was a child. There needed no fathers and mothers to take care of the children, because there was no danger, nor trouble of any kind, and no clothes to be mended, and there was always plenty to eat and drink. Whenever a child wanted his dinner, he found it growing on a tree; and, if he looked at the tree in the morning, he could see the expanding blossom of that night's supper; or, at eventide, he saw the tender bud of to-morrow's breakfast. It was a very pleasant life indeed. No labor to be done, no tasks to be studied; nothing but sports and dances, and sweet voices of children talking, or caroling like birds, or gushing out in merry laughter, throughout the livelong day.

What was most wonderful of all, the children never quarrelled among themselves; neither had they any crying fits; nor, since time first began, had a single one of these little mortals ever gone apart into a corner, and sulked. Oh, what a good time was that to be alive in. The truth is, those ugly little winged monsters, called Troubles, which are now almost as numerous as mosquitoes, had never yet been seen on the earth. It is probable that the very greatest disquietude which a child had ever experienced was Pandora's vexation at not being able to discover the secret of the mysterious box.

This was at first only the faint shadow of a Trouble; but, every day, it grew more and more substantial, until, before a great while, the cottage of Epimetheus and Pandora was less sunshiny than those of the other children.

"Whence can the box have come?" Pandora continually kept saying to herself and to Epimetheus. "And what in the world can be inside of it?"

"Always talking about this box!" said Epimetheus, at last; for he had grown extremely tired of the subject. "I wish, dear Pandora, you would try to talk of something else. Come, let us go and gather some ripe figs, and eat them under the trees, for our supper. And I know a vine that has the sweetest and juiciest grapes you ever tasted."

"Always talking about grapes and figs!" cried Pandora, pettishly.

"Well, then," said Epimetheus, who was a very good-tempered child, like a multitude of children in those days, "let us run out and have a merry time with our playmates."

"I am tired of merry times, and don't care if I never have any more!" answered our pettish little Pandora. "And, besides, I never do have any. This ugly box! I am so taken up with thinking about it all the time. I insist upon your telling me what is inside of it."

"As I have already said, fifty times over, I do not know!" replied Epimetheus, getting a little vexed. "How, then, can I tell you what is inside?"

"You might open it," said Pandora, looking sideways at Epimetheus, "and then we could see for ourselves."

"Pandora, what are you thinking of?" exclaimed Epimetheus.

And his face expressed so much horror at the idea of looking into a box, which had been confided to him on the condition of his never opening it, that Pandora thought it best not to suggest it any more. Still, however, she could not help thinking and talking about the box.

"At least," said she, "you can tell me how it came here."

"It was left at the door," replied Epimetheus, "just before you came, by a person who looked very smiling and intelligent, and who could hardly forbear laughing as he put it down. He was dressed in an odd kind of a cloak, and had on a cap that seemed to be made partly of feathers, so that it looked almost as if it had wings."

"What sort of a staff had he?" asked Pandora.

"Oh, the most curious staff you ever saw!" cried Epimetheus. "It was like two serpents twisting around a stick, and was carved so naturally that I, at first, thought the serpents were alive."

"I know him," said Pandora, thoughtfully. "Nobody else has such a staff. It was Quicksilver; and he brought me hither, as well as the box. No doubt he intended it for me; and, most probably, it contains pretty dresses for me to wear, or toys for you and me to play with, or something very nice for us both to eat!"

"Perhaps so," answered Epimetheus, turning away. "But until Quicksilver comes back and tells us so, we have neither of us any right to lift the lid of the box."

"What a dull boy he is!" muttered Pandora, as Epimetheus left the cottage. "I do wish he had a little more enterprise!"

For the first time since her arrival, Epimetheus had gone out without asking Pandora to accompany him. He went to gather figs and grapes by himself, or to seek whatever amusement he could find, in other society than his little playfellow's. He was tired to death of hearing about the box, and heartily wished that Quicksilver, or whatever was the messenger's name, had left it at some other child's door, where Pandora would never have set eyes on it. So perseveringly as she did babble about this one thing! The box, the box, and nothing but the box! I seemed as if the box were bewitched, and as if the cottage were not big enough to hold it, without Pandora's continually stumbling over it, and making Epimetheus stumble over it likewise, and bruising all four of their shins.

Well, it was really hard that poor Epimetheus should have a box in his ears from morning till night; especially as the little people of the earth were so unaccustomed to vexations, in those happy days, that they knew not how to deal with them. Thus, a small vexation made as much disturbance then, as a far bigger one would in our own times.

After Epimetheus was gone, Pandora stood gazing at the box. She had called it ugly, above a hundred times; but, in spite of all that she had said against it, it was positively a very handsome article of furniture, and would have been quite an ornament to any room in which it should be placed. It was made of a beautiful kind of wood, with dark and rich veins spreading over its surface, which was so highly polished that little Pandora could see her face in it. As the child had no other looking-glass, it is odd that she did not value the box merely on this account.

The edges and corners of the box were carved with most wonderful skill. Around the margin there were figures of graceful men and women, and the prettiest children ever seen, reclining or sporting amid a profusion of flowers and foliage; and these various objects were so exquisitely represented, and were wrought together in such harmony, that flowers, foliage, and human beings seemed to combine into a wreath of mingled beauty. But here and there, peeping forth from behind the carved foliage, Pandora once or twice fancied that she saw a face not so lovely, or something or other that was disagreeable, and which stole the beauty out of all the rest. Nevertheless, on looking more closely, and touching the spot with her finger, she could discover nothing of the kind. Some face, that was really beautiful, had been made to look ugly by her catching a sideway glimpse at it.

The most beautiful face of all was done in what is called high relief, in the centre of the lid. There was nothing else, save the dark, smooth richness of the polished wood, and this one face in the centre, with a garland of flowers about its brow. Pandora had looked at this face a great many times, and imagined that the mouth could smile if it liked, or be grave when it chose, the same as any living mouth. The features, indeed, all wore a very lively and rather mischievous expression, which looked almost as if it needs must burst out of the carved lips, and utter itself in words.

Had the mouth spoken, it would probably have been something like this: —

"Do not be afraid, Pandora! What harm can there be in opening the box? Never mind that poor, simple Epimetheus! You are wiser than he, and have ten times as much spirit. Open the box, and see if you do not find something very pretty!"

The box, I had almost forgotten to say, was fastened; not by a lock, nor by any other such contrivance, but by a very intricate knot of gold cord. There appeared to be no end to this knot, and no beginning. Never was a knot so cunningly twisted, nor with so many ins and outs, which roguishly defied the skilfullest fingers to disentangle them. And yet, by the very difficulty that there was in it, Pandora was the more tempted to examine the knot, and just see how it was made. Two or three times, already, she had stooped over the box, and taken the knot between her thumb and forefinger, but without positively trying to undo it.

"I really believe," said she to herself, "that I begin to see how it was done. Nay, perhaps I could tie it up again, after undoing it. There would be no harm in that, surely. Even Epimetheus would not blame me for that. I need not open the box, and should not, of course, without the foolish boy's consent, even if the knot were untied."

It might have been better for Pandora if she had had a little work to do, or anything to employ her mind upon, so as not to be so constantly thinking of this one subject. But children led so easy a life, before any Troubles came into the world, that they had really a great deal too much leisure. They could not be forever playing at hide-and-seek among the flower-shrubs, or at blind-man's bluff with garlands over their eyes, or at whatever other games had been found out, while Mother Earth was in her babyhood. When life is all sport, toil is the real play. There was absolutely nothing to do. A little sweeping and dusting about the cottage, I suppose, and the gathering of fresh flowers (which were only too abundant everywhere), and arranging them in vases, — and poor little Pandora's day's work was over. And then, for the rest of the day, there was the box!

After all, I am not quite sure that the box was not a blessing to her in its way. It supplied her with such a variety of ideas to think of, and to talk about, whenever she had anybody to listen! When she was in good-humor, she could admire the bright polish of its sides, and the rich border of beautiful faces and foliage that ran all around it. Or, if she chanced to be ill-tempered, she could give it a push, or kick it with her naughty little foot. And many a kick did the box — (but it was a mischievous box, as we shall see, and deserved all it got) — many a kick did it receive. But, certain it is, if it had not been for the box, our active-minded little Pandora would not have known half so well how to spend her time as she now did.

For it was really an endless employment to guess what was inside. What could it be, indeed? Just imagine, my little hearers, how busy your wits would be, if there were a great box in the house, which, as you might have reason to suppose, contained something new and pretty for your Christmas or New-Year's gifts. Do you think that you should be less curious than Pandora? If you were left alone with the box, might you not feel a little tempted to lift the lid? But you would not do it. Oh, fie! No, no! Only, if you thought there were toys in it, it would be so very hard to let slip an opportunity of taking just one peep! I know not whether Pandora expected any toys; for none had yet begun to be made, probably, in those days, when the world itself was one great plaything for the children that dwelt upon it. But Pandora was convinced that there was something very beautiful and valuable in the box; and therefore she felt just as anxious to take a peep as any of these little girls, here around me, would have felt. And, possibly, a little more so; but of that I am not quite so certain.

On this particular day, however, which we have so long been talking about, her curiosity grew so much greater than it usually was, that, at last, she approached the box. She was more than half determined to open it, if she could. Ah, naughty Pandora!

First, however, she tried to lift it. It was heavy; quite too heavy for the slender strength of a child, like Pandora. She raised one end of the box a few inches from the floor, and let it fall again, with a pretty loud thump. A moment afterwards, she almost fancied that she heard something stir inside of the box. She applied her ear as closely as possible, and listened. Positively, there did seem to be a kind of stifled murmur, within! Or was it merely the singing in Pandora's ears? Or could it be the beating of her heart? The child could not quite satisfy herself whether she had heard anything or no. But, at all events, her curiosity was stronger than ever.

As she drew back her head, her eyes fell upon the knot of gold cord.

"It must have been a very ingenious person who tied this knot," said Pandora to herself. "But I think I could untie it nevertheless. I am resolved, at least, to find the two ends of the cord."

So she took the golden knot in her fingers, and pried into its intricacies as sharply as she could. Almost without intending it, or quite knowing what she was about, she was soon busily engaged in attempting to undo it. Meanwhile, the bright sunshine came through the open window; as did likewise the merry voices of the children playing at a distance, and perhaps the voice of Epimetheus among them. Pandora stopped to listen. What a beautiful day it was! Would it not be wiser, if she were to let the troublesome knot alone, and think no more about the box, but run and join her little playfellows, and be happy?

All this time, however, her fingers were half unconsciously busy with the knot; and happening to glance at the flower-wreathed face on the lid of the enchanted box, she seemed to perceive it slyly grinning at her.

"That face looks very mischievous," thought Pandora. "I wonder whether it smiles because I am doing wrong! I have the greatest mind in the world to run away!"

But just then, by the merest accident, she gave the knot a kind of a twist, which produced a wonderful result. The gold cord untwined itself, as if by magic, and left the box without a fastening.

"This is the strangest thing I ever knew!" said Pandora. "What will Epimetheus say? And how can I possibly tie it up again?"

She made one or two attempts to restore the knot, but soon found it quite beyond her skill. It had disentangled itself so suddenly that she could not in the least remember how the strings had been doubled into one another; and when she tried to recollect the shape and appearance of the knot, it seemed to have gone entirely out of her mind. Nothing was to be done, therefore, but to let the box remain as it was until Epimetheus should come in.

"But," said Pandora, "when he finds the knot untied, he will know that I have done it. How shall I make him believe that I have not looked into the box?"

And then the thought came into her naughty little heart, that, since she would be suspected of having looked into the box, she might just as well do so at once. Oh, very naughty and very foolish Pandora! You should have thought only of doing what was right and of leaving undone what was wrong, and not of what your playfellow Epimetheus would have said or believed. And so perhaps she might, if the enchanted face on the lid of the box had not looked so bewitchingly persuasive at her, and if she had not seemed to hear,. more distinctly than before, the murmur of small voices within. She could not tell whether it was fancy or no; but there was quite a little tumult of whispers in her ear, — or else it was her curiosity that whispered, —

"Let us out, dear Pandora, — pray let us out! We will be such nice pretty playfellows for you! Only let us out!"

"What can it be?" thought Pandora. "Is there something alive in the box? Well! — yes — I am resolved to take just one peep! Only one peep; and then the lid shall be shut down as safely as ever! There cannot possibly be any harm in just one little peep!"

But it is now time for us to see what Epimetheus was doing.

This was the first time, since his little playmate had come to dwell with him, that he had attempted to enjoy any pleasure in which she did not partake. But nothing went right; nor was he nearly so happy as on other days. He could not find a sweet grape or a ripe fig (if Epimetheus had a fault, it was a little too much fondness for figs); or, if ripe at all, they were over-ripe, and so sweet as to be cloying. There was no mirth in his heart, such as usually made his voice gush out, of its own accord, and swell the merriment of his companions. In short, he grew so uneasy and discontented, that the other children could not imagine what was the matter with Epimetheus. Neither did he himself know what ailed him any better than they did. For you must recollect that, at the time we are speaking of, it was everybody's nature, and constant habit, to be happy. The world had not yet learned to be otherwise. Not a single soul or body, since these children were first sent to enjoy themselves on the beautiful earth, had ever been sick or out of sorts.

At length, discovering that, somehow or other, he put a stop to all the play, Epimetheus judged it best to go back to Pandora, who was in a humor better suited to his own. But, with a hope of giving her pleasure, he gathered some flowers, and made them into a wreath, which he meant to put upon her head. The flowers were very lovely — roses, and lilies, and orange-blossoms, and a great many more, which left a trail of fragrance behind, as Epimetheus carried them along; and the wreath was put together with as much skill as could reasonably be expected of a boy. The fingers of little girls, it has always appeared to me, are the fittest to twine flower-wreaths; but boys could do it in those days, rather better than they can now.

And here I must mention that a black cloud had been gathering in the sky for some time past, although it had not yet overspread the sun. But, just as Epimetheus reached the cottage door, this cloud began to intercept the sunshine, and thus to make a sudden and sad obscurity.

He entered softly; for he meant, if possible, to steal behind Pandora, and fling the wreath of flowers over her head, before she should be aware of his approach. But, as it happened, there was no need of his treading so very lightly. He might have trod as heavily as he pleased — as heavily as a grown man — as heavily, I was going to say, as an elephant — without much probability of Pandora's hearing his footsteps. She was too intent upon her purpose. At the moment of his entering the cottage, the naughty child had put her hand to the lid, and was on the point of opening the mysterious box. Epimetheus beheld her. If he had cried out, Pandora would probably have withdrawn her hand, and the fatal mystery of the box might never have been known.

But Epimetheus himself, although he said very little about it, had his own share of curiosity to know what was inside. Perceiving that Pandora was resolved to find out the secret, he determined that his playfellow should not be the only wise person in the cottage. And if there were anything pretty or valuable in the box, he meant to take half of it to himself. Thus, after all his sage speeches to Pandora about restraining her curiosity, Epimetheus turned out to be quite as foolish, and nearly as much in fault, as she. So, whenever we blame Pandora for what happened, we must not forget to shake our heads at Epimetheus likewise.

As Pandora raised the lid, the cottage grew very dark and dismal; for the black cloud had now swept quite over the sun, and seemed to have buried it alive. There had, for a little while past, been a low growling and muttering, which all at once broke into a heavy peal of thunder. But Pandora, heeding nothing of all this, lifted the lid nearly upright, and looked inside. It seemed as if a sudden swarm of winged creatures brushed past her, taking flight out of the box, while, at the same instant, she heard the voice of Epimetheus, with a lamentable tone, as if he were in pain.

"Oh, I am stung!" cried he. "I am stung! Naughty Pandora! Why have you opened this wicked box?"

Pandora let fall the lid, and starting up, looked about her to see what had befallen Epimetheus. The thunder-cloud had so darkened the room that she could not very clearly discern what was in it. But she heard a disagreeable buzzing, as if a great many huge flies, or gigantic mosquitoes, or those insects which we call dor-bugs, and pinching-dogs, were darting about. And, as her eyes grew more accustomed to the imperfect light, she saw a crowd of ugly little shapes, with bats' wings looking abominably spiteful, and armed with terribly long stings in their tails. It was one of these that had stung Epimetheus. Nor was it a great while before Pandora herself began to scream, in no less pain and affright than her playfellow, and making a vast deal more hubbub about it. An odious little monster had settled on her forehead, and would have stung her I know not how deeply, if Epimetheus had not run and brushed it away.

Now, if you wish to know what these ugly things might be, which had made their escape out of the box, I must tell you that they were the whole family of earthly Troubles. There were evil Passions; there were a great many species of Cares; there were more than a hundred and fifty Sorrows; there were Diseases, in a vast number of miserable and painful shapes; there were more kinds of Naughtiness than it would be of any use to talk about. In short, everything that has since afflicted the souls and bodies of mankind had been shut up in the mysterious box, and given to Epimetheus and Pandora to be kept safely, in order that the happy children of the world might never be molested by them. Had they been faithful to their trust, all would have gone well. No grown person would ever have been sad, nor any child have had cause to shed a single tear, from that hour until this moment.

But — and you may see by this how a wrong act of any one mortal is a calamity to the whole world — by Pandora's lifting the lid of that miserable box, and by the fault of Epimetheus, too, in not preventing her, these Troubles have obtained a foothold among us, and do not seem very likely to be driven away in a hurry. For it was impossible, as you will easily guess, that the two children should keep the ugly swarm in their own little cottage. On the contrary, the first thing that they did was to fling open the doors and windows, in hopes of getting rid of them, and, sure enough, away flew the winged Troubles all abroad, and so pestered and tormented the small people, everywhere about, that none of them so much as smiled for many days afterwards. And, what was very singular, all the flowers and dewy blossoms

on earth, not one of which had hitherto faded, now began to droop and shed their leaves, after a day or two. The children, moreover, who before seemed immortal in their childhood, now grew older, day by day, and came soon to be youths and maidens, and men and women by and by, and aged people, before they dreamed of such a thing.

Meanwhile, the naughty Pandora, and hardly less naughty Epimetheus, remained in their cottage. Both of them had been grievously stung, and were in a good deal of pain, which seemed the more intolerable to them, because it was the very first pain that had ever been felt since the world began. Of course, they were entirely unaccustomed to it, and could have no idea what it meant. Besides all this, they were in exceedingly bad humor, both with themselves and with one another. In order to indulge it to the utmost, Epimetheus sat down sullenly in a corner with his back towards Pandora; while Pandora flung herself upon the floor and rested her head on the fatal and abominable box. She was crying bitterly, and sobbing as if her heart would break.

Suddenly there was a gentle little tap on the inside of the lid.

"What can that be?" cried Pandora, lifting her head.

But either Epimetheus had not heard the tap, or was too much out of humor to notice it. At any rate, he made no answer.

"You are very unkind," said Pandora, sobbing anew, "not to speak to me!"

Again the tap! It sounded like the tiny knuckles of a fairy's hand, knocking lightly and playfully on the inside of the box.

"Who are you?" asked Pandora, with a little of her former curiosity. "Who are you, inside of this naughty box?"

A sweet little voice spoke from within —

"Only lift the lid, and you shall see."

"No, no," answered Pandora, again beginning to sob; "I have had enough of lifting the lid! You are inside of the box, naughty creature, and there you shall stay! There are plenty of your ugly brothers and sisters already flying about the world. You need never think that I shall be so foolish as to let you out!"

She looked towards Epimetheus as she spoke, perhaps expecting that he would commend her for her wisdom. But the sullen boy only muttered that she was wise a little too late.

"Ah," said the sweet little voice again, "you had much better let me out. I am not like those naughty creatures that have stings in their tails. They are no brothers and sisters of mine, as you would see at once, if you were only to get a glimpse of me. Come, come, my pretty Pandora! I am sure you will let me out!"

And, indeed, there was a kind of cheerful witchery in the tone, that made it almost impossible to refuse anything which this little voice asked. Pandora's heart had insensibly grown lighter at every word that came from within the box. Epimetheus, too, though still in the corner, had turned half round, and seemed to be in rather better spirits than before.

"My dear Epimetheus," cried Pandora, "have you heard this little voice?"

"Yes, to be sure I have," answered he, but in no very good-humor as yet. "And what of it?"

"Shall I lift the lid again?" asked Pandora.

"Just as you please," said Epimetheus. "You have done so much mischief already, that perhaps you may as well do a little more. One other Trouble, in such a swarm as you have set adrift about the world, can make no very great difference."

"You might speak a little more kindly!" murmured Pandora, wiping her eyes.

"Ah, naughty boy!" cried the little voice within the box, in an arch and laughing tone. "He knows he is longing to see me. Come, my dear Pandora, lift up the lid. I am in a great hurry to comfort you. Only let me have some fresh air, and you shall see that matters are not quite so dismal as you think them!"

"Epimetheus," exclaimed Pandora, "come what may, I am resolved to open the box!"

"And, as the lid seems very heavy," cried Epimetheus, running across the room, "I will help you!"

So, with one consent, the two children again lifted the lid. Out flew a sunny and smiling little personage, and hovered about the room, throwing a light wherever she went. Have you never made the sunshine dance into dark corners, by reflecting it from a bit of looking-glass? Well, so looked the winged cheerfulness of this fairy-like stranger, amid the gloom of the cottage. She flew to Epimetheus, and laid the least touch of her finger on the inflamed spot where the Trouble had stung him, and immediately the anguish of it was gone. Then she kissed Pandora on the forehead, and her hurt was cured likewise.

After performing these good offices, the bright stranger fluttered sportively over the children's heads, and looked so sweetly at them, that they both began to think it not so very much amiss to have opened the box, since, otherwise, their cheery guest must have been kept a prisoner among those naughty imps with stings in their tails.

"Pray, who are you, beautiful creature?" inquired Pandora.

"I am to be called Hope!" answered the sunshiny figure. "And because I am such a cheery little body, I was packed into the box, to make amends to the human race for that swarm of ugly Troubles which was destined to be let loose among them. Never fear! we shall do pretty well in spite of them all."

"Your wings are colored like the rainbow!" exclaimed Pandora. "How very beautiful!"

"Yes, they are like the rainbow," said Hope, "Because, glad as my nature is, I am partly made of tears as well as smiles."

"And will you stay with us," asked Epimetheus, "forever and ever?"

"As long as you need me," said Hope, with her pleasant smile — "and that will be as long as you live in the world — I promise never to desert you. There may come times and seasons, now and then, when you will think that I have utterly vanished. But again, and again, and again, when perhaps you least dream of it, you shall see the glimmer of my wings on the ceiling of your cottage. Yes, my dear children, and I know something very good and beautiful that is to be given you hereafter!"

"Oh, tell us," they exclaimed, — "tell us what it is!"

"Do not ask me," replied Hope, putting her finger on her rosy mouth. "But do not despair, even if it should never happen while you live on this earth. Trust in my promise, for it is true."

"We do trust you!" cried Epimetheus and Pandora, both in one breath.

And so they did; and not only they, but so has everybody trusted Hope, that has since been alive. And to tell you the truth, I cannot help being glad — (though, to be sure, it was an uncommonly naughty thing for her to do) — but I cannot help being glad that our foolish Pandora peeped into the box. No doubt — no doubt — the Troubles are still flying about the world,

and have increased in multitude, rather than lessened, and are a very ugly set of imps, and carry most venomous stings in their tails. I have felt them already, and expect to feel them more, as I grow older. But then that lovely and lightsome little figure of Hope! What in the world could we do without her? Hope spiritualizes the earth; Hope makes it always new; and, even in the earth's best and brightest aspect, Hope shows it to be only the shadow of an infinite bliss hereafter!

THE ANGEL

henever a good child dies, an angel descends from heaven, takes the dead child in its arms, spreads out its great white wings, and flies to all the places which were dear to the child, where it gathers a handful of flowers, which are carried up to God and planted. The merciful Father presses all the flowers to his heart; but the flower he likes best he kisses, and then it obtains a voice and can join in the song of the blessed.

That was what an Angel told a dead child whom it was carrying up to heaven; and the child listened as if in a dream, while they visited the places where the child had played, and floated through gardens full of lovely flowers.

"Which shall we take with us to be planted in heaven?" said the child.

There stood a pretty rose-tree there, which an evil hand had broken, so that the boughs, full of great, half-opened buds, hung down withered.

"Poor tree!" exclaimed the child. "Let us take it with us, so that it may bloom in heaven."

And the Angel took it, kissing the child for its thought, whereby it opened its eyes.

They gathered some gorgeous flowers, but also some simple ones, as, for instance, the common daisy and the wild pansy.

"Now we have flowers," said the child; and the Angel nodded, but still they did not fly up to heaven.

It was night, and everything was silent. They were still in the great city, floating through one of the narrowest streets, where there lay bundles of straw, bits of crockery, rags, and an old hat; for the people had moved that day.

And the Angel pointed among all these remains to the fragment of an old flower-pot and a little lump of mould which had fallen out of it, but was still held together by the roots of a common field-flower. It was of no value, and had therefore been thrown into the street.

"We will take this with us," said the Angel. "I will tell you stories while we fly."

So they flew, and the Angel told this story: —

"Down in that narrow street, in the low cellar, lived a poor boy who was ill. He had been in bed since he was quite a baby, and when he was at his best could only crawl about in the little room on crutches; that was all. For a few days during the summer the rays of the sun fell for half an hour into the porch of the cellar, and when the little boy sat there in the sun, looking at the red blood in his emaciated hands, which he held before the sun, it was said, "To-day he has been out." He knew the woods in their lovely greenness only through the first branch of the beech-tree brought him in the spring by the son of a neighbor; and this he fastened over his bed, and then dreamt that he was under the trees where the sun shone and the birds sang. One spring day his friend brought him some field-flowers, among which was one with a root, and he placed it in a flower-pot in the window, close to his bed. It became the loveliest garden to the child — his only treasure on earth. He watered and tended it, and took every care that it should have every ray of the sun, to the very last, in the window. And the flower grew in his dreams, for it bloomed for him and gladdened his eye; towards it he turned when God called him to his heavenly rest.

"For a year he has been with God, and for a year the flower has stood in the window, unheeded and forgotten, till it has been cast into the street as useless. And this is the poor, withered flower in our bouquet, for it has afforded more happiness and delight than the most gorgeous in the garden of the Queen."

"But how do you know all this?" said the child whom the Angel was carrying up to heaven.

"I know it," said the Angel, "for I myself was that suffering little boy on crutches. I have not forgotten my flower."

And the child opened its eyes wide and looked into the lovely and

happy face of the Angel; and in the same moment they floated into heaven, where joy and gladness reign. And the God-Father pressed the little child to his heart, when it obtained wings like the other Angel, and flew about with it hand-in-hand. Then the Lord pressed the flowers to his heart; but the poor common field-flower he kissed, and it had a voice, and could sing with the other angels who floated about the Lord — some quite near, others behind them, and some far, far away; but they were all equally happy. And they all sang, great and small, the good child and the poor field-flower, which had lain withered in the dust among the rubbish in the dark, narrow street.

BLUE BEARD

There was in former times a very rich gentleman. He had fine town and country houses; his dishes and plates were all of gold or silver; his rooms were hung with embroidered tapestry; his chairs and sofas were covered with the finest damask, and his carriages were all gilt in a grand style. But, unfortunately, this gentleman had a blue beard, which made him so very ugly and frightful, that none of the ladies in the parts where he lived would venture to go into his company.

Now a certain lady of rank, who lived very near him, had two daughters, both eminently beautiful. Blue Beard asked her to bestow one of them upon him for his wife, leaving it to herself to choose which of the two it should be. Both the young ladies said, over and over again, that they would never marry a man with a blue beard; yet, in order to be as civil as they could, each of them said that she only objected to him because she was loath to hinder her sister from such an honourable match. The truth of the matter was, besides the circumstance of his blue beard, they knew that he had already married several wives, and nobody could tell what had ever become of any of them.

Blue Beard, in order to gain their favour, asked the lady and her daughters, with some of their friends and acquaintances, to accompany him to one of his country villas; the invitation was accepted, and a whole week was passed in nothing but parties for hunting and fishing, music, dancing, feasts, and picnic excursions; no one ever thought of going to bed, and the nights were spent in merry-makings of all kinds. In short, the time rolled on in so much pleasure that the youngest of the two sisters began to think that the beard was not so very blue, and that the gentleman who owned it was a very civil and obliging person. Shortly after their return home, the marriage was celebrated.

About a month after the wedding, Blue Beard told his wife that he was obliged to leave her for six weeks at least, as he had some business of importance to transact in the country. He desired her to be sure to indulge herself in every kind of pleasure during his absence; to invite as many of her friends as she liked, to take them into the country if she chose, and to treat them with all sorts of dainties.

"Here," said he, "are the keys of the two large store-rooms; this is the key of the great box that contains the best gold and silver plate, which we use only for company; this unlocks the strong box in which I keep my money, and this is the key of my diamond and jewel caskets. Here also is the master-key to all the rooms in the house; as for this little key, it belongs to the closet at the end of the long gallery on the ground-floor. I give you free leave," he continued, "to open and do what you like with all the rest; but this little closet I forbid you to enter, or even to put the key into the lock, on any account whatever. If you do not obey me in this particular, but open the closet-door, I warn you to expect the most terrible of punishments from my anger."

The wife promised to obey his orders in the most punctual manner, and Blue Beard, after tenderly embracing her and bidding her adieu, stepped into his carriage and drove away.

When Blue Beard was gone, the neighbours and friends of his wife did not wait to be invited, so eager was their curiosity to behold all the riches and rarities that she had become mistress of by her marriage; for none of them had dared to go to the wedding, or to visit her since, on account of the bridegroom's blue beard, which inspired them all with terror. As soon as they arrived, they ran over Blue Beard's house from room to room, from closet to closet, from store-room to store-room, observing with surprise and delight that each one they came to was richer and more splendid than the one they had just quitted. When they came to the suite of drawing-rooms, they could not sufficiently admire the costly grandeur of the tapestry, the gorgeous beds, the rich sofas, the rare cabinets, the brilliant chandeliers, the luxurious chairs and tables, and the noble mirrors; the frames of these last were of silver gilt, superbly chased, and the plates, some being of the finest glass and others sheets of burnished silver, reflected the beholder's figure from head to foot. In a word, nothing could exceed the costly elegance of Blue Beard's furniture, and his wife's acquaintances failed not to admire and envy her good fortune. The wife, meanwhile, was far from thinking about the fine speeches they made to her, and was intent only upon exploring the secrets of the closet on the ground-floor that her husband had so strictly forbidden her to open.

At last her curiosity became so great that, without thinking how rude it would be to leave her guests, she slipped away down a private staircase that led to the gallery, and her haste was so great that she was two or three times in danger of falling and breaking her neck. When she reached the closet-door, she paused to reflect a minute or two on the order her husband had given her, and to consider that her disobedience might perhaps be attended by fatal consequences. But curiosity to know what the closet contained assailed her so powerfully that she was unable to resist its impulse, and, resolved to gratify it at all hazards, with a trembling hand she put the little key into the lock and turned it, and the door immediately flew wide open.

The room being partially darkened by thick blinds before the windows, she could at first see nothing distinctly; but in a short time, her eyes growing accustomed to the twilight, she perceived that the floor was covered with clotted blood, in which were lying the heads of several dead women, parallel with the walls. These were Blue Beard's unfortunate former wives, whom he had killed one after another.

On beholding this terrible sight, the poor young wife was ready to faint with fear, and, in her confusion, the key of the closet, which she had drawn from the lock, fell from her hand on the floor.

When she had a little recovered from her fright, she picked up the key, locked the door, and hastened back to her own room, to prepare to amuse her company; but her agitation was so great that her attempts to quell it were vain. Taking notice that the key of the closet had got stained with blood in falling on the floor, she endeavoured to cleanse it by wiping it with her handkerchief; but the blood was immovable: in vain she washed it, and even scoured it with sand and brick-dust; the blood still remained on the key, in spite of all her efforts. Well it might, for the key was a fairy key, and there was no means of thoroughly cleansing it; as fast as the blood was rubbed off one side, it made its appearance on the other.

Early that same evening Blue Beard returned home, saying that, before he had got many miles on his journey, he had received letters advising him that the affair he was about to attend in person was settled to his advantage without his presence. His wife said everything she could think of to make him believe she was transported with joy at his sudden return. The next morning he asked her for the keys; she gave them to him, but her hand trembled so violently that Blue Beard was at no loss to guess all that had taken place.

"How is it," said he, "that the key of the closet on the ground-floor is not here with the others?"

"I must have left it upstairs on my dressing-table," said the wife.

"Do not fail," replied Blue Beard, "to return it to me by-and-by."

After walking backwards and forwards several times, to make belief that she was looking for the key, she at last gave it up with reluctance. Blue Beard, having taken it into his hands and examined it, asked his wife, "How came this blood on the key?"

"I am sure I do not know," answered the poor terrified lady, turning as pale as a corpse.

"You do not know!" returned Blue Beard sternly; "but I know, well enough. You have been into the closet on the ground-floor. Very well, madam! You shall go there again, for your disobedience, and take your place among the ladies you saw."

The poor young lady threw herself on her knees before her husband, weeping bitterly and displaying all the signs of a true repentance for having disobeyed him, and supplicated his pardon for her first fault in the most affecting terms. Her beauty and distress would have melted a rock; but Blue Beard's heart was harder than a rock.

"No, madam," said he, "you must die this very minute."

"Alas! if I must die," answered she, regarding her relentless husband with streaming eyes, "at least give me a short time to say my prayers."

"You shall have half a quarter of an hour," retorted the cruel Blue Beard, "but not a second more."

When Blue Beard had left her to herself, she called aloud to her sister, and said, "Sister Anne" (that was her sister's name), "prithee run up to the top of the tower and see if my brothers are in sight; they promised to visit me to-day. If you see them, make signs to them to gallop hither as fast as they can."

The sister immediately ascended to the battlements of the tower, and the poor trembling lady cried out to her every moment: "Anne! Sister Anne! Do you see anyone coming?"

"I see nothing," answered Sister Anne, "but the sun which makes a dust, and the grass which looks green."

Blue Beard, in the meantime, with a large naked sword in his hand, called out as loud as he could bawl: "Come down at once, or I will fetch you!"

"Grant me one moment, I beseech you," replied his wife, and then called softly to her sister: "Anne! Sister Anne! do you see anyone coming?"

"Alas!" answered Sister Anne, "I see nothing but the sun which makes a dust, and the grass which looks green."

"Come down, I say, this very moment," vociferated Blue Beard, "or I will come and fetch you."

"I am coming," sobbed the wretched wife, calling again to her sister in a low voice: "Anne! Sister Anne! do you see anyone coming?"

"I see," answered Sister Anne, "a large cloud of dust a little to the right."

"Do you think it is my brothers?" asked the wife.

"Alas! no, dear sister," answered Anne; "it is only a flock of sheep."

"Will you, or will you not, come down, madam?" roared Blue Beard, foaming with rage.

"Only one short moment more," answered his wife. Then she again called out, for the last time: "Anne! Sister Anne! Do you see anyone coming?"

"I see," replied Sister Anne, "two men approaching on horseback; but they are still a great distance off."

"Thank God!" exclaimed the poor wife, "it is my brothers."

"I beckon them to make haste," said Sister Anne, "as well I can."

Blue Beard now bellowed out so loudly for his wife to come downstairs that his voice shook the whole house. The poor young lady, with dishevelled hair and tears streaming from her eyes, now came down, and begged him on her knees to spare her life. "It is all of no avail," said Blue Beard, "you shall die."

Seizing her by the hair with one hand, and raising his sword over her head with the other, he was now preparing to strike off her head, when the unfortunate young lady, turning her dying looks on her unrelenting husband, entreated him to stay his hand a moment while she repeated one short prayer. "No, no," said Blue Beard, "recommend your soul to God, for you have not another moment to live."

While he was steadying his arm to make sure of his blow, a loud knocking was heard at the gates, which made Blue Beard pause a moment to see who it was. The gates flew open, and two officers, in full uniform, rushed into the mansion; they drew their swords and hastened up to Blue Beard, who, knowing

them at a glance to be his wife's brothers, one a dragoon and the other a hussar, tried to escape from their presence. But the brothers pursued him so nimbly that they overtook him before he had gone twenty steps, and, passing their swords through his body, laid him dead at their feet. The poor wife, almost as dead as her husband, was unable for some time to embrace and thank her brothers for their timely rescue.

As Blue Beard left no heirs, his wife inherited all his immense wealth. She bestowed part of her vast fortune, as a marriage dowry, on her sister Anne, who was shortly afterwards united to a young gentleman who had long loved her. Some of the money she laid out in the purchase of captain's commissions in their respective regiments for her two brothers; and with the residue she endowed a worthy and noble-minded young man, to whom she was shortly afterwards married, and whose kind treatment soon made her forget the cruel usage she had received from Blue Beard.

THE WHITE CAT

Once upon a time there was a king who had three sons, who were all so clever and brave that he began to be afraid that they would want to reign over the kingdom before he was dead. Now the King, though he felt that he was growing old, did not at all wish to give up the government of his kingdom while he could still manage it very well, so he thought the best way to live in peace would be to divert the minds of his sons by promises which he could always get out of when the time came for keeping them.

So he sent for them all, and, after speaking to them kindly, he added:

"You will quite agree with me, my dear children, that my great age makes it impossible for me to look after my affairs of state as carefully as I once did. I begin to fear that this may affect the welfare of my subjects, therefore I wish that one of you should succeed to my crown; but in return for such a gift as this, it is only right that you should do something for me. Now, as I think of retiring into the country, it seems to me that a pretty, lively, faithful little dog would be very good company for me; so, without any regard for your ages, I promise that the one who brings me the most beautiful little dog shall succeed me at once."

The three Princes were greatly surprised by their father's sudden fancy for a little dog, but as it gave the two younger ones a chance they would not otherwise have had of being king, and as the eldest was too polite to make any objection, they accepted the commission with pleasure. They bade farewell to the King, who gave them presents of silver and precious stones, and appointed to meet them at the same hour, in the same place, after a year had passed, to see the little dogs they had brought for him.

Then they went together to a castle which was about a league from the city, accompanied by all their particular friends, to whom they gave a grand banquet, and the three brothers promised to be friends always, to share whatever good fortune befell them, and not to be parted by any envy or jealousy; and so they set out, agreeing to meet at the same castle at the appointed time, to present themselves before the King together. Each one took a different road, and the two eldest met with many adventures; but it is about the youngest that you are going to hear. He was young, and gay, and handsome, and knew everything that a prince ought to know; and as for his courage, there was simply no end to it.

Hardly a day passed without his buying several dogs — big and little, greyhounds, mastiffs, spaniels, and lapdogs. As soon as he had bought a pretty one he was sure to see a still prettier, and then he had to get rid of all the others and buy that one, as, being alone, he found it impossible to take thirty or forty thousand dogs about with him. He journeyed from day to day, not knowing where he was going, until at last, just at nightfall, he reached a great, gloomy forest. He did not know his way, and, to make matters worse, it began to thunder, and the rain poured down. He took the first path he could find, and after walking for a long time he fancied he saw a faint light, and began to hope that he was coming to some cottage where he might find shelter for the night. At length, guided by the light, he reached the door of the most splendid castle he could have imagined. This door was of gold covered with carbuncles, and it was the pure red light which shone from them that had shown him the way through the forest. The walls were of the finest porcelain in all the most delicate colors, and the Prince saw that all the stories he had ever read were pictured upon them; but as he was terribly wet, and the rain still fell in torrents, he could not stay to look about any more, but came back to the golden door. There he saw a deer's foot hanging by a chain of diamonds, and he began to wonder who could live in this magnificent castle.

"They must feel very secure against robbers," he said to himself. "What is to hinder anyone from cutting off that chain and digging out those carbuncles, and making himself rich for life?"

He pulled the deer's foot, and immediately a silver bell sounded and the door flew open, but the Prince could see nothing but numbers of hands in the air, each holding a torch. He was so much surprised that he stood quite still, until he felt himself pushed forward by other hands, so that, though he was somewhat uneasy, he could not help going on. With his hand on his sword, to be prepared for whatever might happen, he entered a hall paved with lapis-lazuli, while two lovely voices sang:

> The hands you see floating above
> Will swiftly your bidding obey;
> If your heart dreads not conquering Love,
> In this place you may fearlessly stay.

The Prince could not believe that any danger threatened him when he was welcomed in this way, so, guided by the mysterious hands, he went toward a door of coral, which opened of its own accord, and he found himself in a vast hall of mother-of-pearl, out of which opened a number of other rooms, glittering with thousands of lights, and full of such beautiful pictures and precious things that the Prince felt quite bewildered. After passing through sixty rooms, the hands that conducted him stopped, and the Prince saw a most comfortable-looking arm-chair drawn up close to the chimney-corner; at the same moment the fire lighted itself, and the pretty, soft, clever hands took off the Prince's wet, muddy clothes, and presented him with fresh ones made of the richest stuffs, all embroidered with gold and emeralds. He could not help admiring everything he saw, and the deft way in which the hands waited on him, though they sometimes appeared so suddenly that they made him jump.

When he was quite ready — and I can assure you that he looked very different from the wet and weary Prince who had stood outside in the rain, and pulled the deer's foot — the hands led him to a splendid room, upon the walls of which were painted the histories of Puss in Boots and a number of other famous cats. The table was laid for supper with two golden plates, and golden spoons and forks, and the sideboard was covered with dishes and glasses of crystal set with precious stones. The Prince was wondering who the second place could be for, when suddenly in came about a dozen cats carrying guitars and rolls of music, who took their places at one end of the room, and under the direction of a cat who beat time with a roll of paper began to mew in every imaginable key, and to draw their claws across the strings of the guitars, making the strangest kind of music that could be heard. The Prince hastily stopped up his ears, but even then the sight of these comical musicians sent him into fits of laughter.

"What funny thing shall I see next?" he said to himself, and instantly the door opened, and in came a tiny figure covered by a long black veil. It was conducted by two cats wearing black mantles and carrying swords, and a large party of cats followed, who brought in cages full of rats and mice.

The Prince was so much astonished that he thought he must be dreaming, but the little figure came up to him and threw back its veil, and he saw that it was the loveliest little white cat it is possible to imagine. She looked very young and very sad, and in a sweet little voice that went straight to his heart she said to the Prince:

"King's son, you are welcome; the Queen of the Cats is glad to see you."

"Lady Cat," replied the Prince, "I thank you for receiving me so kindly, but surely you are no ordinary pussy-cat? Indeed, the way you speak and the magnificence of your castle prove it plainly."

"King's son," said the White Cat, "I beg you to spare me these compliments, for I am not used to them. But now," she added, "let supper be served, and let the musicians be silent, as the Prince does not understand what they are saying."

So the mysterious hands began to bring in the supper, and first they put on the table two dishes, one containing stewed pigeons and the other a fricassee of fat mice. The sight of the latter made the Prince feel as if he could not enjoy his supper at all; but the White Cat, seeing this, assured him that the dishes intended for him were prepared in a separate kitchen, and he might be quite certain that they contained neither rats nor mice; and the Prince felt so sure that she would not deceive him that he had no more hesitation in beginning. Presently he noticed that on the little paw that was next him the White Cat wore a bracelet containing a portrait, and he begged to be allowed to look at it. To his great surprise he found it represented an extremely handsome young man, who was so like himself that it might have been his own portrait! The White Cat sighed as he looked at it, and seemed sadder than ever, and the Prince dared not ask any questions for fear of displeasing her; so he began to talk about other things, and found that she was interested in all the subjects he cared for himself, and seemed to know quite well what was going on in the world. After supper they went

into another room, which was fitted up as a theatre, and the cats acted and danced for their amusement, and then the White Cat said good-night to him, and the hands conducted him into a room he had not seen before, hung with tapestry worked with butterflies' wings of every color; there were mirrors that reached from the ceiling to the floor, and a little white bed with curtains of gauze tied up with ribbons. The Prince went to bed in silence, as he did not quite know how to begin a conversation with the hands that waited on him, and in the morning he was awakened by a noise and confusion outside of his window, and the hands came and quickly dressed him in hunting costume. When he looked out, all the cats were assembled in the courtyard, some leading greyhounds, some blowing horns, for the White Cat was going out hunting. The hands led a wooden horse up to the Prince, and seemed to expect him to mount it, at which he was very indignant; but it was no use for him to object, for he speedily found himself upon its back, and it pranced gaily off with him.

The White Cat herself was riding a monkey, which climbed even up to the eagles' nests when she had a fancy for the young eaglets. Never was there a pleasanter hunting party, and when they returned to the castle the Prince and the White Cat supped together as before, but when they had finished she offered him a crystal goblet, which must have contained a magic draught, for, as soon as he had swallowed its contents, he forgot everything, even the little dog that he was seeking for the King, and only thought how happy he was to be with the White Cat! And so the days passed, in every kind of amusement, until the year was nearly gone. The Prince had forgotten all about meeting his brothers: he did not even know what country he belonged to; but the White Cat knew when he ought to go back, and one day she said to him:

"Do you know that you have only three days left to look for the little dog for your father, and your brothers have found lovely ones?"

Then the Prince suddenly recovered his memory, and cried:

"What can have made me forget such an important thing? My whole fortune depends upon it; and even if I could in such a short time find a dog pretty enough to gain me a kingdom, where should I find a horse who would carry me all that way in three days?" And he began to be very vexed. But the White Cat said to him: "King's son, do not trouble yourself; I am your friend, and will make everything easy for you. You can still stay here for

a day, as the good wooden horse can take you to your country in twelve hours."

"I thank you, beautiful Cat," said the Prince; "but what good will it do me to get back if I have not a dog to take to my father?"

"See here," answered the White Cat, holding up an acorn; "there is a prettier one in this than in the Dogstar!"

"Oh! White Cat dear," said the Prince, "how unkind you are to laugh at me now!"

"Only listen," she said, holding the acorn to his ear.

And inside it he distinctly heard a tiny voice say: "Bow-wow!"

The Prince was delighted, for a dog that can be shut up in an acorn must be very small indeed. He wanted to take it out and look at it, but the White Cat said it would be better not to open the acorn till he was before the King, in case the tiny dog should be cold on the journey. He thanked her a thousand times, and said good-by quite sadly when the time came for him to set out.

"The days have passed so quickly with you," he said, "I only wish I could take you with me now."

But the White Cat shook her head and sighed deeply in answer.

After all, the Prince was the first to arrive at the castle where he had agreed to meet his brothers, but they came soon after, and stared in amazement when they saw the wooden horse in the courtyard jumping like a hunter.

The Prince met them joyfully, and they began to tell him all their adventures; but he managed to hide from them what he had been doing, and even led them to think that a turnspit dog which he had with him was the one he was bringing for the King. Fond as they all were of one another, the two eldest could not help being glad to think that their dogs certainly had a better chance. The next morning they started in the same chariot. The elder brothers carried in baskets two such tiny, fragile dogs that they hardly dared to touch them. As for the turnspit, he ran after the chariot, and got so covered with mud that one could hardly see what he was like at all. When they reached the palace everyone crowded round to welcome them as they went into the King's great hall; and when the two brothers presented their little dogs nobody could decide which was the prettier. They were already arranging between themselves to share the kingdom equally, when the youngest stepped forward, drawing from his pocket the acorn the White Cat had given him. He opened it quickly, and there upon a white cushion they saw a dog so small that it could easily have been put through a ring. The Prince laid it upon the ground, and it got up at once and began to dance. The King did not know what to say, for it was impossible that anything could be prettier than this little creature. Nevertheless, as he was in no hurry to part with his crown, he told his sons that, as they had been so successful the first time, he would ask them to go once again, and seek by land and sea for a piece of muslin so fine that it could be drawn through the eye of a needle. The brothers were not very willing to set out again, but the two eldest consented because it gave them another chance, and they started as before. The youngest again mounted the wooden horse, and rode back at full speed to his beloved White Cat. Every door of the castle stood wide open, and every window and turret was illuminated, so it looked more wonderful than before. The hands hastened to meet him, and led the wooden horse off to the stable, while he hurried in to find the White Cat. She was asleep in a little basket on a white satin cushion, but she very soon started up when she heard the Prince, and was overjoyed at seeing him once more.

"How could I hope that you would come back to me, King's son?" she said. And then he stroked and petted her, and told her of his successful journey, and how he had come back to ask her help, as he believed that it was impossible to find what the King demanded. The White Cat looked serious, and said she must think what was to be done, but that, luckily, there were some cats in the castle who could spin very well, and if anybody could manage it they could, and she would set them the task herself.

And then the hands appeared carrying torches, and conducted the Prince and the White Cat to a long gallery which overlooked the river, from the windows of which they saw a magnificent display of fireworks of all sorts; after which they had supper, which the Prince liked even better than the fireworks, for it was very late, and he was hungry after his long ride. And so the days passed quickly as before; it was impossible to feel dull with the White Cat, and she had quite a talent for inventing new amusements — indeed, she was cleverer than a cat has any right to be. But when the Prince asked her how it was that she was so wise, she only said:

"King's son, do not ask me; guess what you please. I may not tell you anything."

The Prince was so happy that he did not trouble himself at all about the time, but presently the White Cat told him that the year was gone, and that he need not be at all anxious about the piece of muslin, as they had made it very well.

"This time," she added, "I can give you a suitable escort"; and on looking out into the courtyard the Prince saw a superb chariot of burnished gold, enameled in flame color with a thousand different devices. It was drawn by twelve snow-white horses, harnessed four abreast; their trappings were flame-colored velvet, embroidered with diamonds. A hundred chariots followed, each drawn by eight horses, and filled with officers in splendid uniforms, and a thousand guards surrounded the procession. "Go!" said the White Cat, "and when you appear before the King in such state he surely will not refuse you the crown which you deserve. Take this walnut, but do not open it until you are before him, then you will find in it the piece of stuff you asked me for."

"Lovely Blanchette," said the Prince, "how can I thank you properly for all your kindness to me? Only tell me that you wish it, and I will give up forever all thought of being king, and will stay here with you always."

"King's son," she replied, "it shows the goodness of your heart that you should care so much for a little white cat, who is good for nothing but to catch mice; but you must not stay."

So the Prince kissed her little paw and set out. You can imagine how fast he traveled when I tell you that they reached the King's palace in just half the time it had taken the wooden horse to get there. This time the Prince was so late that he did not try to meet his brothers at their castle, so they thought he could not be coming, and were rather glad of it, and displayed their pieces of muslin to the King proudly, feeling sure of success. And indeed the stuff was very fine, and would go through the eye of a very large needle; but the King, who was only too glad to make a difficulty, sent for a particular needle, which was kept among the Crown jewels, and had such a small eye that everybody saw at once that it was impossible that the muslin should pass through it. The Princes were angry, and were beginning to complain that it was a trick, when suddenly the trumpets sounded and the youngest Prince came in. His father and brothers were quite astonished at his magnificence, and after he had greeted them he took the walnut from his pocket and opened it, fully expecting to find the piece of muslin, but instead there was only a hazel-nut. He cracked it, and there lay a cherry-stone. Everybody was looking on, and the King was chuckling to himself at the idea of finding the piece of muslin in a nutshell.

However, the Prince cracked the cherry-stone, but everyone laughed when he saw it contained only its own kernel. He opened that and found a grain of wheat, and in that was a millet seed. Then he himself began to wonder, and muttered softly:

"White Cat, White Cat, are you making fun of me?"

In an instant he felt a cat's claw give his hand quite a sharp scratch, and hoping that it was meant as an encouragement he opened the millet seed, and drew out of it a piece of muslin four hundred ells long, woven with the loveliest colors and most wonderful patterns; and when the needle was brought it went through the eye six times with the greatest ease! The King turned pale, and the other Princes stood silent and sorrowful, for nobody could deny that this was the most marvelous piece of muslin that was to be found in the world.

Presently the King turned to his sons, and said, with a deep sigh:

"Nothing could console me more in my old age than to realize your willingness to gratify my wishes. Go then once more, and whoever at the end of a year can bring back the loveliest princess shall be married to her, and shall, without further delay, receive the crown, for my successor must certainly be married." The Prince considered that he had earned the kingdom fairly twice over, but still he was too well bred to argue about it, so he just went back to his gorgeous chariot, and, surrounded by his escort, returned to the White Cat faster than he had come. This time she was expecting him, the path was strewn with flowers, and a thousand braziers were burning scented woods which perfumed the air. Seated in a gallery from which she could see his arrival, the White Cat waited for him. "Well, King's son," she said, "here you are once more, without a crown." "Madam," said he, "thanks to your generosity I have earned one twice over; but the fact is that my father is so loth to part with it that it would be no pleasure to me to take it."

"Never mind," she answered, "it's just as well to try and deserve it. As you must take back a lovely princess with you next time I will be on the look-out for one for you. In the meantime let us enjoy ourselves; to-night I have ordered a battle between my cats and the river rats, on purpose to amuse you." So this year slipped away even more pleasantly than the preceding ones. Sometimes the Prince could not help asking the White Cat how it was she could talk.

"Perhaps you are a fairy," he said. "Or has some enchanter changed you into a cat?"

But she only gave him answers that told him nothing. Days go by so quickly when one is very happy that it is certain the Prince would never have thought of its being time to go back, when one evening as they sat together the White Cat said to him that if he wanted to take a lovely princess home with him the next day he must be prepared to do what she told him.

"Take this sword," she said, "and cut off my head!"

"I!" cried the Prince, "I cut off your head! Blanchette darling, how could I do it?"

"I entreat you to do as I tell you, King's son," she replied.

The tears came into the Prince's eyes as he begged her to ask him anything but that — to set him any task she pleased as a proof of his devotion, but to spare him the grief of killing his dear Pussy. But nothing he could say altered her determination, and at last he drew his sword, and desperately, with a trembling hand, cut off the little white head. But imagine his astonishment and delight when suddenly a lovely princess stood before him, and, while he was still speechless with amazement, the door opened and a goodly company of knights and ladies entered, each carrying a cat's skin! They hastened with every sign of joy to the Princess, kissing her hand and congratulating her on being once more restored to her natural shape. She received them graciously, but after a few minutes begged that they would leave her alone with the Prince, to whom she said:

"You see, Prince, that you were right in supposing me to be no ordinary cat. My father reigned over six kingdoms. The Queen, my mother, whom he loved dearly, had a passion for traveling and exploring, and when I was only a few weeks old, she obtained his permission to visit a certain mountain of which she had heard many marvelous tales, and set out, taking with her a number of her attendants. On the way they had to pass near an old castle belonging to the fairies. Nobody had ever been into it, but it was reported to be full of the most wonderful things, and my mother remembered to have heard that the fairies had in their garden such fruits as were to be seen and tasted nowhere else. She began to wish to try them for herself, and turned her steps in the direction of the garden. On arriving at the door, which blazed with gold and jewels, she ordered her servants to knock loudly, but it was useless; it seemed as if all the inhabitants of the castle must be asleep or dead. Now the more difficult it became to obtain the fruit, the more the Queen was determined that have it she would. So she ordered that they should bring ladders, and get over the wall into the garden; but though the wall did not look very high, and they tied the ladders together to make them very long, it was quite impossible to get to the top.

"The Queen was in despair, but as night was coming on she ordered that they should encamp just where they were, and went to bed herself, feeling quite ill, she was so disappointed. In the middle of the night, she was suddenly awakened, and saw to her surprise a tiny, ugly old woman seated by her bedside, who said to her:

" 'I must say that we consider it somewhat troublesome of your Majesty to insist upon tasting our fruit; but to save you annoyance, my sisters and I will consent to give you as much as you can carry away, on one condition — that is, that you shall give us your little daughter to bring up as our own.'

" 'Ah! my dear madam,' cried the Queen, 'is there nothing else that you will take for the fruit? I will give you my kingdoms willingly.'

" 'No,' replied the old fairy, 'we will have nothing but your little daughter. She shall be as happy as the day is long, and we will give her everything that is worth having in fairy-land, but you must not see her again until she is married.'

" 'Though it is a hard condition,' said the Queen, 'I consent, for I shall certainly die if I do not taste the fruit, and so I should lose my little daughter either way.'

"So the old fairy led her into the castle, and, though it was still the middle of the night, the Queen could see plainly that it was far more beautiful than she had been told, which you can easily believe, Prince," said the White Cat, "when I tell you that it was this castle that we are now in. 'Will you gather the fruit yourself, Queen?' said the old fairy, 'or shall I call it to come to you?'

" 'I beg you to let me see it come when it is called,' cried the Queen; 'that will be something quite new.' The old fairy whistled twice, then she cried:

" 'Apricots, peaches, nectarines, cherries, plums, pears, melons, grapes, apples, oranges, lemons, gooseberries, strawberries, raspberries, come!'

"And in an instant they came tumbling in one over another, and yet they were neither dusty nor spoilt, and the Queen found them quite as good as she had fancied them. You see they grew upon fairy trees.

"The old fairy gave her golden baskets in which to take the fruit away, and it was as much as four hundred mules could carry. Then she reminded the Queen of her agreement, and led her back to the camp, and next morning she went back to her kingdom, but before she had gone very far she began to repent her bargain, and when the King came out to meet her she looked so sad that he guessed that something had happened, and asked what was the matter. At first the Queen was afraid to tell him, but when, as soon as they reached the palace, five frightful little dwarfs were sent by the fairies to fetch me, she was obliged to confess what she had promised. The King was very angry, and had the Queen and myself shut up in a great tower and safely guarded, and drove the little dwarfs out of his kingdom; but the fairies sent a great dragon who ate up all the people he met, and whose breath burnt up everything as he passed through the country; and at last, after trying in vain to rid himself of this monster, the King, to save his subjects, was obliged to consent that I should be given up to the fairies. This time they came themselves to fetch me, in a chariot of pearl drawn by sea-horses, followed by the dragon, who was led with chains of diamonds. My cradle was placed between the old fairies, who loaded me with caresses, and away we whirled through the air to a tower which they had built on purpose for me. There I grew up surrounded with everything that was beautiful and rare, and learning everything that is ever taught to a princess, but without any companions but a parrot and a little dog, who could both talk; and receiving every day a visit from one of the old fairies, who came mounted upon the dragon.

"One day, however, as I sat at my window I saw a handsome young prince, who seemed to have been hunting in the forest which surrounded my prison, and who was standing and looking up at me. When he saw that I observed him, he saluted me with great deference. You can imagine that I was delighted to have some one new to talk to, and in spite of the height of my window our conversation was prolonged till night fell, then my prince reluctantly bade me farewell. But after that he came again many times, and at last I consented to marry him, but the question was how was I to escape from my tower. The fairies always supplied me with flax for my spinning, and by great diligence I made enough cord for a ladder that would reach to the foot of my tower; but, alas! just as my prince was helping me to descend it, the crossest and ugliest of the old fairies flew in. Before he had time to defend himself my unhappy lover was swallowed up by the dragon. As for me, the fairies, furious at having their plans defeated, for they intended me to marry the king of the dwarfs, and I utterly refused, changed me into a white cat. When they brought me here I found all the lords and ladies of my father's court awaiting me under the same enchantment, while the people of lesser rank had been made invisible, all but their hands.

"As they laid me under the enchantment the fairies told me all my history, for until then I had quite believed that I was their child, and warned me that my only chance of regaining my natural form was to win the love of a prince who resembled in every way my unfortunate lover."

"And you have won it, lovely Princess," interrupted the Prince.

"You are indeed wonderfully like him," resumed the Princess — "in voice, in features, and everything; and if you really love me all my troubles will be at an end."

"And mine too," cried the Prince, throwing himself at her feet, "if you will consent to marry me."

"I love you already better than anyone in the world," she said; "but now it is time to go back to your father, and we shall hear what he says about it."

So the Prince gave her his hand and led her out, and they mounted the chariot together; it was even more splendid than before, and so was the whole company. Even the horses' shoes were of rubies with diamond nails, and I suppose that is the first time such a thing was ever seen.

As the Princess was as kind and clever as she was beautiful, you may imagine what a delightful journey the Prince found it, for everything the Princess said seemed to him quite charming.

When they came near the castle where the brothers were to meet, the Princess got into a chair carried by four of the guards; it was hewn out of one splendid crystal, and had silken curtains, which she drew round her that she might not be seen.

The Prince saw his brothers walking upon the terrace, each with a lovely princess, and they came to meet him, asking if he had also found a wife. He said that he had found something much rarer — a white cat! At which they laughed very much, and asked him if he was afraid of being eaten up by mice in the palace. And then they set out together for the town. Each prince and princess rode in a splendid carriage; the horses were decked with plumes of feathers, and glittered with gold. After them came the youngest prince, and last of all the crystal chair, at which everybody looked with admiration and curiosity. When the courtiers saw them coming they hastened to tell the King.

"Are the ladies beautiful?" he asked anxiously.

And when they answered that nobody had ever before seen such lovely princesses he seemed quite annoyed.

However, he received them graciously, but found it impossible to choose between them.

Then turning to his youngest son, he said:

"Have you come back alone, after all?"

"Your Majesty," replied the Prince, "will find in that crystal chair a little white cat, which has such soft paws, and mews so prettily, that I am sure you will be charmed with it."

The King smiled, and went to draw back the curtains himself, but at a touch from the Princess the crystal shivered into a thousand splinters, and there she stood in all her beauty; her fair hair floated over her shoulders and was crowned with flowers, and her softly falling robe was of the purest white. She saluted the King gracefully, while a murmur of admiration rose from all around.

"Sire," she said, "I am not come to deprive you of the throne you fill so worthily. I have already six kingdoms, permit me to bestow one upon you, and upon each of your sons. I ask nothing but your friendship, and your consent to my marriage with your youngest son; we shall still have three kingdoms left for ourselves."

The King and all the courtiers could not conceal their joy and astonishment, and the marriage of the three Princes was celebrated at once. The festivities lasted several months, and then each king and queen departed to their own kingdom and lived happily ever after.

THE FIVE WISE WORDS OF THE GURU

Once there lived a handsome young man named Ram Singh, who, though a favourite with everyone, was unhappy because he had a scold for a step-mother. All day long she went on talking, until the youth was driven so distracted that he determined to go away somewhere and seek his fortune. No sooner had he decided to leave his home than he made his plans, and the very next morning he started off with a few clothes in a wallet, and a little money in his pocket.

But there was one person in the village to whom he wished to say good-bye, and that was a wise old guru, or teacher, who had taught him much. So he turned his face first of all towards his master's hut, and before the sun was well up was knocking at his door. The old man received his pupil affectionately; but he was wise in reading faces, and saw at once that the youth was in trouble.

"My son," said he, "what is the matter?"

"Nothing, father," replied the young man, "but I have determined to go into the world and seek my fortune."

"Be advised," returned the guru, "and remain in your father's house; it is better to have half a loaf at home than to seek a whole one in distant countries."

But Ram Singh was in no mood to heed such advice, and very soon the old man ceased to press him.

"Well," said he at last, "if your mind is made up I suppose you must have your way. But listen carefully, and remember five parting counsels which I will give you; and if you keep these no evil shall befall you. First — always obey without question the orders of him whose service you enter; second — never speak harshly or unkindly to anyone; third — never lie; fourth — never try to appear the equal of those above you in station; and fifth — wherever you go, if you meet those who read or teach from the holy books, stay and listen, if but for a few minutes, that you may be strengthened in the path of duty."

Then Ram Singh started out upon his journey, promising to bear in mind the old man's words.

After some days he came to a great city. He had spent all the money which he had at starting, and therefore resolved to look for work however humble it might be. Catching sight of a prosperous-looking merchant standing in front of a shop full of grain of all kinds, Ram Singh went up to him and asked whether he could give him anything to do. The merchant gazed at him so long that the young man began to lose heart, but at length he answered:

"Yes, of course; there is a place waiting for you."

"What do you mean?" asked Ram Singh.

"Why," replied the other, "yesterday our rajah's chief wazir dismissed his body servant and is wanting another. Now you are just the sort of person that he needs, for you are young and tall, and handsome; I advise you to apply there."

Thanking the merchant for this advice, the young man set out at once for the wazir's house, and soon managed, thanks to his good looks and appearance, to be engaged as the great man's servant.

One day, soon after this, the rajah of the place started on a journey and the chief wazir accompanied him. With them was an army of servants and attendants, soldiers, muleteers, camel-drivers, merchants with grain and stores for man and beast, singers to make entertainment by the way and musicians to accompany them, besides elephants, camels, horses, mules, ponies, donkeys, goats, and carts and wagons of every kind and description, so that it seemed more like a large town on the march than anything else.

Thus they travelled for several days, till they entered a country that was like a sea of sand, where the swirling dust floated in clouds, and men and beasts were half choked by it. Towards the close of that day they came to a village, and when the headmen hurried out to salute the rajah and to pay him their respects, they began, with very long and serious faces, to explain that, whilst they and all that they had were of course at the disposal of the rajah, the coming of so large a company had nevertheless put them into a dreadful difficulty because they had never a well nor spring of water in their country; and they had no water to give drink to such an army of men and beasts!

Great fear fell upon the host at the words of the headmen, but the rajah merely told the wazir that he must get water somehow, and that settled the matter so far as *he* was concerned. The wazir sent off in haste for all the oldest men in the place, and began to question them as to whether there were no wells near by.

They all looked helplessly at each other, and said nothing; but at length one old grey-beard replied:

"Truly, Sir Wazir, there is, within a mile or two of this village, a well which some former king made hundreds of years ago. It is, they say, great and inexhaustible, covered in by heavy stone-work and with a flight of steps leading down to the water in the very bowels of the earth; but no man ever goes near it because it is haunted by evil spirits, and it is known that whoso disappears down the well shall never be seen again."

The wazir stroked his beard and considered a moment. Then he turned to Ram Singh who stood behind his chair.

"There is a proverb," said he, "that no man can be trusted until he has been tried. Go you and get the rajah and his people water from this well."

Then there flashed into Ram Singh's mind the first counsel of the old guru — *'Always obey without question the orders of him whose service you enter.'* So he replied at once that he was ready, and left to prepare for his adventure. Two great brazen vessels he fastened to a mule, two lesser ones he bound upon his shoulders, and thus provided he set out, with the old villager for his guide. In a short time they came to a spot where some big trees towered above the barren country, whilst under their shadow lay the dome of an ancient building. This the guide pointed out as the well, but excused himself from going further as he was an old man and tired, and it was already nearly sunset, so that he must be returning home. So Ram Singh bade him farewell, and went on alone with the mule.

Arrived at the trees, Ram Singh tied up his beast, lifted the vessels from his shoulder, and having found the opening of the well, descended by a flight of steps which led down into the darkness. The steps were broad white slabs of alabaster which gleamed in the shadows as he went lower and lower. All was very silent. Even the sound of his bare feet upon the pavement seemed to wake an echo in that lonely place, and when one of the vessels which he carried slipped and fell upon the steps it clanged so loudly that he jumped at the noise. Still he went on, until at last he reached a wide pool of sweet water, and there he washed his jars with care before he filled them, and began to remount the steps with the lighter vessels, as the big ones were so heavy he could only take up one at a time. Suddenly, something moved above him, and looking up he saw a great giant standing on the stairway! In one hand he held clasped to his heart a dreadful looking mass of bones, in the other was a lamp which cast long shadows about the walls, and made him seem even more terrible than he really was.

"What think you, O mortal," said the giant, "of my fair and lovely wife?" And he held the light towards the bones in his arms and looked lovingly at them.

Now I must tell you that this poor giant had had a very beautiful wife, whom he had loved dearly; but, when she died, her husband refused to believe in her death, and always carried her about long after she had become nothing but bones. Ram Singh of course did not know of this, but there came to his mind the second wise saying of the guru, which forbade him to speak harshly or inconsiderately to others; so he replied:

"Truly, sir, I am sure you could find nowhere such another."

"Ah, what eyes you have!" cried the delighted giant, "you at least can see! I do not know how often I have slain those who insulted her by saying she was but dried bones! You are a fine young man, and I will help you."

So saying, he laid down the bones with great tenderness, and snatching up the huge brass vessels, carried them up again, and replaced them with such ease that it was all done by the time that Ram Singh had reached the open air with the smaller ones.

"Now," said the giant, "you have pleased me, and you may ask of me one favour, and whatever you wish I will do it for you. Perhaps you would like me to show you where lies buried the treasure of dead kings?" he added eagerly.

But Ram Singh shook his head at the mention of buried wealth.

"The favour that I would ask," said he, "is that you will leave off haunting this well, so that men may go in and out and obtain water."

Perhaps the giant expected some favour more difficult to grant, for his face brightened, and he promised to depart at once; and as Ram Singh went off through the gathering darkness with his precious burden of water, he beheld the giant striding away with the bones of his dead wife in his arms.

Great was the wonder and rejoicing in the camp when Ram Singh returned with the water. He never said anything, however, about his adventure with the giant, but merely told the rajah that there was nothing to prevent the well being used; and used it was, and nobody ever saw any more of the giant.

The rajah was so pleased with the bearing of Ram Singh that he ordered the wazir to give the young man to him in exchange for one of his own servants. So Ram Singh became the rajah's attendant; and as the days went by the king became more and more delighted with the youth because, mindful of the old guru's third counsel, he was always honest and spoke the truth. He grew in favour rapidly, until at last the rajah made him his treasurer, and thus he reached a high place in the court and had wealth and power in his hands. Unluckily the rajah had a brother who was a very bad man; and this brother thought that if he could win the young treasurer over to himself he might by this means manage to steal little by little any of the king's treasure which he needed. Then, with plenty of money, he could bribe the soldiers and some of the rajah's counsellors, head a rebellion, dethrone and kill his brother, and reign himself instead. He was too wary, of course, to tell Ram Singh of all these wicked plans; but he began by flattering him whenever he saw him, and at last offered him his daughter in marriage. But Ram Singh remembered the fourth counsel of the old guru — never to try to appear the equal of those above him in station — therefore he respectfully declined the great honour of marrying a princess. Of course the prince, baffled at the very beginning of his enterprise, was furious, and determined to work Ram Singh's ruin, and entering the rajah's presence he told him a story about Ram Singh having spoken insulting words of his sovereign and of his daughter. What it was all about nobody knew, and, as it was not true, the wicked prince did not know either; but the rajah grew very angry and red in the face as he listened, and declared that until the treasurer's head was cut off neither he nor the princess nor his brother would eat or drink.

"But," added he, "I do not wish anyone to know that this was done by my desire, and anyone who mentions the subject will be severely punished." And with this the prince was forced to be content.

Then the rajah sent for an officer of his guard, and told him to take some soldiers and ride at once to a tower which was situated just outside the town, and if anyone should come to inquire when the building was going to be finished, or should ask any other questions about it, the officer must chop his head off, and bring it to him. As for the body, that could be buried on the spot. The old officer thought these instructions rather odd, but it was no business of his, so he saluted, and went off to do his master's bidding.

Early in the morning the rajah, who had not slept all night, sent for Ram Singh, and bade him go to the new hunting-tower, and ask the people there how it was getting on and when it was going to be finished, and to hurry back with the answer! Away went Ram Singh upon his errand, but, on the road, as he was passing a little temple on the outskirts of the city, he heard someone inside reading aloud; and, remembering the guru's fifth counsel, he just stepped inside and sat down to listen for a minute. He did not mean to stay longer, but became so deeply interested in the wisdom of the teacher, that he sat, and sat, and sat, while the sun rose higher and higher.

In the meantime, the wicked prince, who dared not disobey the rajah's command, was feeling very hungry; and as for the princess, she was quietly crying in a corner waiting for the news of Ram Singh's death, so that she might eat her breakfast.

Hours passed, and stare as he might from the window no messenger could be seen.

At last the prince could bear it no longer, and hastily disguising himself so that no one should recognise him, he jumped on a horse and galloped out to the hunting-tower, where the rajah had told him that the execution was to take place. But, when he got there, there was no execution going on. There were only some men engaged in building, and a number of soldiers idly watching them. He forgot that he had disguised himself and that no one would know him, so, riding up, he cried out:

"Now then, you men, why are you idling about here instead of finishing what you came to do? When is it to be done?"

At his words the soldiers looked at the commanding officer, who was standing a little apart from the rest. Unperceived by the prince he made a slight sign, a sword flashed in the sun, and off flew a head on the ground beneath!

As part of the prince's disguise had been a thick beard, the men did not recognise the dead man as the rajah's brother; but they wrapped the head in a cloth, and buried the body as their commander bade them. When this was ended, the officer took the cloth, and rode off in the direction of the palace.

Meanwhile the rajah came home from his council, and to his great surprise found neither head nor brother awaiting him; as time passed on, he became uneasy, and thought that he had better go himself and see what the matter was. So ordering his horse he rode off alone.

It happened that, just as the rajah came near to the temple where Ram Singh still sat, the young treasurer, hearing the sound of a horse's hoofs, looked over his shoulder and saw that the rider was the rajah himself! Feeling much ashamed of himself for having forgotten his errand, he jumped up and hurried out to meet his master, who reined up his horse, and seemed very surprised (as indeed he was) to see *him* . At that moment there arrived the officer of the guard carrying his parcel. He saluted the rajah gravely, and, dismounting, laid the bundle in the road and began to undo the wrappings, whilst the rajah watched him with wonder and interest. When the last string was undone, and the head of his brother was displayed to his view, the rajah sprang from his horse and caught the soldier by the arm. As soon as he could speak he questioned the man as to what had occurred, and little by little a dark suspicion darted through him. Then, briefly telling the soldier that he had done well, the rajah drew Ram Singh to one side, and in a few minutes learned from him how, in attending to the guru's counsel, he had delayed to do the king's message.

In the end the rajah found from some papers, the proofs of his dead brother's treachery; and Ram Singh established his innocence and integrity. He continued to serve the rajah for many years with unswerving fidelity; and married a maiden of his own rank in life, with whom he lived happily; dying at last honoured and loved by all men. Sons were born to him; and, in time, to them also he taught the five wise sayings of the old guru.

THE STEADFAST TIN SOLDIER

here were once five-and-twenty tin soldiers, who were all brothers, for they were born together of an old tin spoon. They had guns at the shoulder, looked straight before them, and their uniform was very pretty, being red and blue. The very first word they heard in this world "Tin soldiers," was when the lid was taken off the box in which they lay; and that was exclaimed by a little boy who was clapping his hands, the tin soldiers being his birthday present. He stood them up on the table; each one was like the other, only one being different, having only one leg, as he had been cast last and there was no more tin; but he stood nevertheless as firmly on his one leg as the others on their two, and it is of him we shall tell.

On the table where they stood there was a lot of other playthings; but that which attracted the eye most was a pretty castle made of cardboard. Through the little windows you could see right into the rooms, and outside stood tiny trees around a little looking-glass, which was meant for a lake, and which reflected some wax swans upon it. It was all so very pretty; but still prettier was a little maiden, standing in the open door, and cut from cardboard; but she had on a dress of the finest muslin, and a little blue sash across her shoulders, in the middle of which was fastened a glittering tinsel star as big as her face. The little maiden stretched out both her arms, for she was a dancer, and she raised one leg so high that the Tin Soldier could not see it, so he thought that she too had only one leg like himself.

"That would be just the wife for me," he thought; "but she is high-born, and lives in a castle, while I have only a box, and *that* there are twenty-five of us to share. It is not a fit place for her, but I will nevertheless try to make her acquaintance." And he laid himself down behind a snuff-box on the table, whence he could have a real good look at the pretty little lady, who continued to stand on one leg without overbalancing herself.

At night the rest of the tin soldiers were put into the box, and the family in the house went to bed. Then the playthings began to play among themselves at giving "at homes," dances, and go to war, so that the tin soldiers began to kick in their box, as they wanted to share the fun; but they could not get the lid off. The nut-crackers turned summersaults while the pencil danced a hornpipe on the slate, and there was such a noise that the canary woke and began to join in, and that in verse too. The only two who remained quiet were the Tin Soldier and the little Dancer; she stood still erect on the tip of her toe, with her arms stretched out, and he as firmly on his one leg; but he did not take his eyes off her for an instant.

Just then the clock struck twelve, and Bang! the lid flew off the snuff-box. There was, however, no snuff in it, only a little black imp like a "Jack-in-the-box."

"Tin Soldier," said the imp, "you keep your eyes to yourself!" But the Soldier pretended not to hear him.

"Well, you just wait till to-morrow," said the imp.

The next morning, as soon as the children were up, the Tin Soldier was placed on the window-ledge; and, whether it was the imp or the draught — anyhow, the window suddenly flew open, and the Soldier fell headlong from the second story into the street. It was a frightful fall; he held his leg straight upwards and landed on his shako, with his gun embedded between two paving-stones.

The servant and the little boy went down at once to find him; but though they nearly trod upon him they could not see him. Had the Tin Soldier called out, "I am here!" they would have found him, no doubt; but he did not consider it soldier-like to shout while in uniform.

It began to rain, the drops falling faster and faster, and it soon came down in torrents.

When the rain was over, two street-urchins came along, one of whom exclaimed, "Look! there lies a Tin Soldier; let us give him a sail in the gutter."

And they made a boat out of a piece of newspaper, put the soldier into it, and so he sailed down the gutter, both boys running alongside, clapping

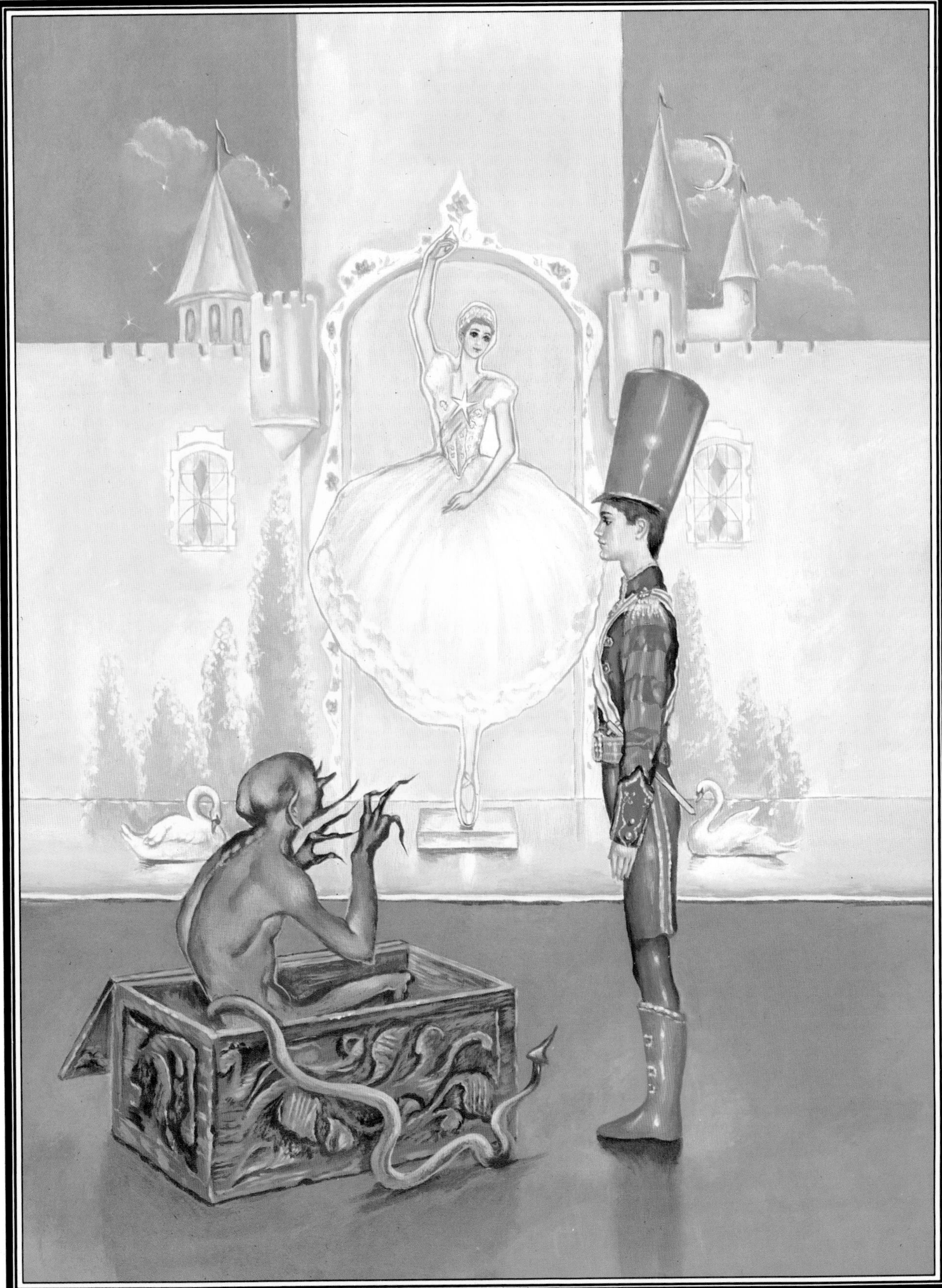

their hands. Oh, how high the waves ran in the gutter, and how strong the current was! But it had been pouring down. The paper boat bobbed up and down, and sometimes spun round so fearfully that the Soldier trembled; but he remained firm, and, not moving a muscle and looking straight before him, kept his gun at the shoulder.

Suddenly the boat drifted under a broad crossing and it became as dark as in the box.

"Where am I going to now, I wonder?" he thought. "I am sure this is the imp's doing. However, if only the little girl was in the boat with me it might really be twice as dark."

Now a large water-rat appeared, which lived under the crossing.

"Have you a pass?" it asked. "Hand it over!" But the Tin Soldier did not say a word, and only clasped his gun firmer. The boat shot along, and the rat followed. Oh, how fearfully it ground its teeth, while calling out to bits of wood and straw, "Stop him! Stop him! he has not paid toll, and he has not shown a pass."

But the current became stronger and stronger; the Tin Soldier now saw daylight where the crossing ceased, but he heard also a roaring noise which might well terrify the bravest. Only imagine; where the crossing ceased, the water in the gutter fell straight into a big canal — a descent as dangerous as that of a waterfall to us.

Now he was so near it he could not stop the boat, and down it went, but the poor Tin Soldier remained as firm as he possibly could; nobody could say that he even blinked his eyes.

The boat spun round three or four times, filled nearly to the edge, and was on the point of sinking. The Tin Soldier was in water up to his neck, while the boat sank deeper and deeper; the paper became more and more undone, and now the water was above the head of the Soldier. At that moment he thought of the pretty little Dancer, whom he should never see again. Now the paper broke, he fell through, and was in the same instant swallowed by a big fish.

Oh, how dark it was in there! much darker than under the crossing; and so little room too; but the Tin Soldier remained steadfast, lying full length with his gun in his arm.

The fish jumped about in the most violent manner; but all of a sudden it became quiet, and something like a ray of light penetrated into it. The

light became quite distinct, and somebody said aloud, "A Tin Soldier!"

The fish had been caught, sold in the fish-market, and carried into the kitchen, where the cook was cutting it up with a big knife. She took him with her two fingers and carried him to the sitting-room, where everybody wished to see the remarkable being who had travelled about in the stomach of a fish; but the Tin Soldier was not at all proud.

They placed him on the table, and — wonder of wonders! — the Tin Soldier was in the same room as before; he saw the same children, and the same playthings on the table. The fine castle and the pretty little Dancer were still there; she was still on her one leg, with the other high in the air; she too was firm. The Tin Soldier was so affected he could have cried, but that would not have been soldier-like. He looked at her, and she at him, but neither said anything.

In the next moment one of the little boys threw the Soldier, without giving any reason, right into the fire; it was, no doubt, the imp's doing again.

The Tin Soldier stood in the full glare, and felt a heat quite dreadful; but whether it was the fire or love he knew not. He had quite lost his colors, but nobody could tell whether on the journey or through grief. He looked at the little maiden, and she at him; he felt he was melting, but still he stood firm with his gun at his shoulder. Just then a door was opened, and the draught catching the Dancer, she flew like a sylph right into the fire where the Soldier stood, blazed up, and disappeared.

The Tin Soldier had now melted into a lump, and when the servant the next morning cleared out the ashes, she found him in the form of a tin heart, while of the Dancer only the tinsel star remained, and that was burned quite black.

THE FISHERMAN AND HIS WIFE

A fisherman once lived contentedly with his wife in a little hut near a lake, and he went every day to throw his line into the water.

One day after angling for a long time without even a bite, the line suddenly sank to the bottom, and when he pulled it up again there was a large flounder hanging to the end of it.

"Oh, dear!" exclaimed the fish; "good fisherman, let me go, I pray you; I am not a real fish, but a prince in disguise. I shall be of no use to you, for I am not good to eat. Put me back again into the water and let me swim away."

"Ah," said the man, "you need not make such a disturbance. I would rather let a flounder who can speak swim away than keep it."

With these words he placed the fish back again in the water, and it sank to the bottom, leaving a long streak of blood behind it. Then the fisherman rose up and went home to his wife in the hut.

"Husband," said the wife, "have you caught anything to-day?"

"I caught a flounder," he replied, "who said he was an enchanted prince; so I threw him back into the water, and let him swim away."

"Did you not wish?" she asked.

"No," he said; "what should I wish for?"

"Why, at least for a better hut than this dirty place. How unlucky you did not think of it! He would have promised you whatever you asked for. However, go and call him now; perhaps he will answer you."

The husband did not like this task at all; he thought it was nonsense.

However, to please his wife, he went and stood by the sea. When he saw how green and dark it looked, he felt much discouraged, but made up a rhyme and said:

Flounder, flounder, in the sea,
Come, I pray, and talk to me;
For my wife, Dame Isabel,
Sent me here a tale to tell.

Then the fish came swimming up to the surface, and said: "What do you want with me?"

"Ah," said the man, "I caught you and let you go again to-day, without wishing; and my wife says I ought to have wished, for she cannot live any longer in such a miserable hut as ours, and she wants a better one."

"Go home, man," said the fish; "your wife has all she wants."

So the husband went home, and there was his wife, no longer in her dirty hovel, but sitting at the door of a neat little cottage, looking very happy.

She took her husband by the hand and said: "Come in, and see how much better it is than the other old hut."

So he followed her in, and found a beautiful parlor, and a bright stove in it, a soft bed in the bedroom, and a kitchen full of earthenware, and tin and copper vessels for cooking, looking so bright and clean, and all of the very best. Outside was a little farm-yard, with hens and chickens running about, and, beyond, a garden containing plenty of fruit and vegetables.

"See," said the wife; "is it not delightful?"

"Ah, yes," replied her husband, "as long as it is new you will be quite contented; but after that, we shall see."

"Yes, we shall see," said the wife.

A fortnight passed, and the husband felt quite happy, till one day his wife startled him by saying, "Husband, after all, this is only a cottage, much too small for us, and the yard and the garden cover very little ground. If the fish is really a prince in disguise, he could very well give us a larger house. I should like, above all things, to live in a large castle built of stone. Go to thy fish and ask him to build us a castle."

"Ah, wife," he said, "this cottage is good enough for us; what do we want of a castle?"

"Go along," she replied; "the flounder will be sure to give us what you ask."

"Nay, wife," said he; "the fish gave us the cottage at first, but if I go again he may be angry."

"Never mind," she replied; "he can do what I wish easily, and I have no doubt he will; so go and try."

The husband rose to go with a heavy heart; he said to himself, "This is not right," and when he reached the sea he noticed that the water was now a dark blue, yet very calm; so he began his old song:

Flounder, flounder, in the sea,
Come, I pray, and talk to me;
For my wife, Dame Isabel,
Wishes what I fear to tell.

"Now, then, what do you want?" said the fish, lifting his head above the water.

"Oh, dear!" said the fisherman in a frightened tone, "my wife wants to live in a great stone castle."

"Go home, man, and you will find her there," was the reply.

The husband hastened home, and where the cottage had been there stood a great stone castle, and his wife tripped down the steps, saying: "Come with me, and I will show you what a beautiful dwelling we have now!"

So she took him by the hand and led him into the castle, through halls of marble, while numbers of servants stood ready to usher them through folding-doors into rooms where the walls were hung with tapestry and the furniture was of silk and gold. From these they went into other rooms equally elegant, where crystal looking-glasses hung on the walls, and the chairs and tables were of rosewood and marble. The soft carpets sank beneath the footstep, and rich ornaments were arranged about the rooms.

Outside the castle was a large court-yard in which were stables and cow-sheds, horses and carriages, all of the most expensive kind. Beyond this was a beautiful garden full of rare flowers and delicious fruit, besides several acres of field and park land, in which deer, oxen, and sheep were grazing — all, indeed, that the heart could wish was here.

"Well," said the wife, "is not this beautiful?"

"Yes," replied her husband, "and you will think so as long as the humor lasts, and then, I suppose, you will want something more."

"We must think about that," she replied, and then they went to bed.

Not many mornings after this the fisherman's wife rose early. It was just daybreak, and she stood looking out, with her arms akimbo, over the beautiful country that lay before her. Her husband did not stir, and presently she exclaimed: "Get up, husband, and come to the window! Look here, ought you not to be king of all this land? Then I should be queen. Go and tell the fish I want you to be king."

"Ah, wife," he replied, "I don't want to be king. I can't go and ask that."

"Well," she replied, "if you don't care about being king, I wish to be queen, so go and tell the fish what I say."

"It's no use, wife; I cannot."

"Why not? Come, there's a good man, go at once; I must be queen!"

The husband turned away in a sorrowful mood. "It is not right" he said; "it is not right." However, he went, and as he stood on the seashore, he noticed that the water looked quite dark and rough, while the waves foamed and dashed against the shore as if they were angry. But still he said:

Flounder, flounder, in the sea,
Come, I pray, and talk to me;
For my wife, Dame Isabel,
Wishes what I fear to tell.

"What!" cried the fish, rising to the surface, "she is not content, and she wants to be queen? Very well, then; go home, and you will find her so."

When he got near home he found the castle had disappeared, and he saw at a distance a palace, which seemed to grow larger as he approached it. At one end was a large tower, and a noble terrace in front. A sentinel stood at the gates, and a band of soldiers, with drums and trumpets, were performing martial music. On arriving at the palace, he found it was built of precious marble. Within no expense had been spared. The furniture was of the most precious materials, and the curtains and carpets fringed with gold. The husband passed through the doors into a state apartment of immense size, and there sat his wife upon a lofty throne of gold and precious stones. She had a crown of gold upon her head, and a golden scepter in her hand adorned with jewels. On each side of her stood six pages in a row, each one a head taller than the one next to him. He went up to his wife, and said: "Ah, wife, so you are queen now!"

"Yes," she said, "I am queen."

He stood looking at her for a long time till at last he spoke again. "Well, wife, now that you are queen, we have nothing left to wish for; we must give up wishing."

"No, indeed," she replied, "I am not yet satisfied. Time and tide wait for no man, nor will they wait for me. I am as impatient as ever. Go to your enchanted prince again and tell him I want to be empress."

"Empress!" cried the husband. "It is beyond his power, I am certain; the empress has the highest place in the kingdom."

"What!" she replied, "don't you know that I am queen, and that you must obey me, although you are my husband? Go at once; if the prince in disguise can make a queen, he can also make an empress."

So the husband went away muttering to himself, "To keep on wishing in this way is not good; I am certain the fish will put an end to it this time."

When he reached the shore the sea was quite black, and the waves rushed so furiously over the rocks that he was terrified, but he contrived to repeat his wild verse again, saying:

Flounder, flounder, in the sea,
Come, I pray, and talk to me;
For my wife, Dame Isabel,
Wishes what I fear to tell.

Up came the fish.

"Well," he said, "what does she want now?"

"Ah!" said the husband timidly, "she wants to be empress."

"Go home, man," he replied. "She has her wish."

And on his return he found his wife acting as empress in a palace of marble, with alabaster statues, and gold, and pearls; and soldiers, and lords and barons bowing to her; but she was not satisfied even now, and at last told her husband that she wished to be the pope, and that he must go to the fish and tell him so.

"No," he said, "that is impossible. The pope is the head of the Church. You cannot have that wish."

"But I will be pope!" she exclaimed.

So he was obliged to go, and when he reached the shore the sea was running mountains high, and roaring and beating against the shores, and it was such terrible weather that the sky looked quite black.

However, he ventured to call up the fish with the old song, and told him of his wife's wish.

"Go home," he said. "Your wife is pope."

He turned to go back, but what a change he found: the palace had vanished, and in its place stood a large cathedral surrounded by marble pillars.

On a high throne sat his wife, with thousands of lights around her, dressed in robes embroidered with gold, and wearing a large golden crown on her head. Candles of all kinds stood near her, some as thick as a tower, others as small as a rushlight, while emperors, kings, and nobles kneeled at her footstool and kissed her slippers.

"Well, wife," said her husband, "so you are pope?"

"Yes," she said. "I am."

He stood still for a time watching her, and at length he remarked: "You cannot be higher than the pope, so I suppose now you are content?"

"I am not quite sure," she said. But when evening came, and they retired to rest, she could not sleep for thinking of what she should next wish for. Her husband slept soundly, for he had tired himself the day before; but she rose even before the day broke, and stood at the window to watch the sun rise.

It was a beautiful sight, and she exclaimed as she watched it. "Oh, if I only had the power to make the sun rise! Husband, wake up," she added, pushing him in the ribs with her elbows; "wake up, and go and tell the enchanted prince that I wish to be equal to the Creator, and make the sun rise."

The husband was so frightened at this that he tumbled out of bed, and exclaimed: "Ah, wife, what didst thou say?"

She repeated the words.

Her husband fell on his knees before her. "Don't ask me to do this; I cannot!" he cried, but she flew into a rage, and drove him from the house.

The poor fisherman went down to the shore in terror, for a dreadful storm had arisen, and he could scarcely stand on his feet. Ships were wrecked, boats tossed to and fro, and rocks rolled into the sea.

In his terror and confusion he heard a voice from amid the storm:

"Your wife wishes to be equal to the Creator. Go home, man, and find her again in her dirty hovel by the sea!"

He went home, to find the glories, the riches, and the palaces vanished, and his wife sitting in the old hut, an example of the consequences of impious ambition.

CINDERELLA OR THE LITTLE GLASS SLIPPER

Once there was a gentleman who married, for his second wife, the proudest and most haughty woman that was ever seen. She had, by a former husband, two daughters of her own humour and they were indeed exactly like her in all things. He had likewise, by another wife, a young daughter, but of unparalleled goodness and sweetness of temper, which she took from her mother, who was the best creature in the world.

No sooner were the ceremonies of the wedding over, but the step-mother began to show herself in her colours. She could not bear the good qualities of this pretty girl; and the less, because they made her own daughters appear the more odious. She employed her in the meanest work of the house; she scoured the dishes, tables, etc., and scrubbed Madam's chamber, and those of Misses, her daughters; she lay up in a sorry garret, upon a wretched straw-bed, while her sisters lay in fine rooms, with floors all inlaid, upon beds of the very newest fashion, and where they had looking-glasses so large, that they might see themselves at their full length, from head to foot.

The poor girl bore all patiently, and dared not tell her father, who would have rattled her off; for his wife governed him entirely. When she had done her work, she used to go into the chimney-corner, and sit down among cinders and ashes, which made her commonly be called Cinder-breech; but the youngest, who was not so rude and uncivil as the eldest, called her Cinderella. However, Cinderella, notwithstanding her mean apparel, was a hundred times handsomer than her sisters, though they were always dressed very richly.

It happened that the King's son gave a ball, and invited all persons of fashion to it. Our young misses were also invited; for they cut a very grand figure among the quality. They were mightily delighted at this invitation, and wonderfully busy in choosing out such gowns, petticoats, and headclothes as might best become them. This was a new trouble to Cinderella; for it was she who ironed her sisters' linen, and plaited their ruffles; they talked all day long of nothing but how they should be dressed. "For my part," said the eldest, "I will wear my red velvet suit, with French trimming." "And I," said the youngest, "shall only have my usual petticoat; but then, to make amends for that, I will put on my gold-flowered manteau, and my diamond stomacher, which is far from being the most ordinary one in the world." They sent for the best tire-woman they could get, to make up their head-dresses, and adjust their double-pinners[1], and they had their red brushes, and patches from the fashionable maker.

Cinderella was likewise called up to them to be consulted in all these matters, for she had excellent notions, and advised them always for the best, nay and offered her services to dress their heads, which they were very willing she should do. As she was doing this, they said to her:

"Cinderella, would you not be glad to go to the ball?"

"Ah!" said she, "you only jeer at me; it is not for such as I am to go thither."

"Thou art in the right of it," replied they, "it would make the people laugh to see a Cinder-breech at a ball."

Any one but Cinderella would have dressed their heads awry, but she was very good, and dressed them perfectly well. They were almost two days without eating, so much they were transported with joy; they broke above a dozen of laces in trying to be laced up close, that they might have a fine slender shape, and they were continually at their looking-glass. At last the happy day came; they went to Court, and Cinderella followed them with her eyes as long as she could, and when she had lost sight of them she fell a-crying.

Her godmother, who saw her all in tears, asked her what was the matter.

"I wish I could — I wish I could — " She was not able to speak the rest, being interrupted by her tears and sobbing.

This godmother of hers, who was a Fairy, said to her:

"Thou wishest thou couldest go to the ball, is it not so?"

"Y—es," cried Cinderella, with a great sigh.

"Well," said her godmother, "be but a good girl, and I will contrive that thou shalt go." Then she took her into her chamber, and said to her:

"Run into the garden, and bring me a pumpkin."

Cinderella went immediately to gather the finest she could get, and brought it to her godmother, not being able to imagine how this pumpkin could make her go to the ball. Her godmother scooped out all the inside of it, leaving nothing but the rind; which done, she struck it with her wand, and the pumpkin was instantly turned into a fine coach.

She then went to look into her mouse-trap, where she found six mice all alive, and ordered Cinderella to lift up a little trap-door, when giving each mouse, as it went out, a little tap with her wand, the mouse was at that moment turned into a fair horse, which altogether made a very fine set of six horses of a beautiful mouse-coloured dapple-grey.

Being at a loss for a coachman, "I will go and see," says Cinderella, "if there be never a rat in the rat-trap, that we may make a coachman of him."

"Thou art in the right," replied her godmother; "go and look."

Cinderella brought the trap to her, and in it there were three huge rats. The Fairy made choice of one of the three, which had the largest beard, and, having touched him with her wand, he was turned into a fat jolly coachman, who had the smartest whiskers eyes ever beheld.

After that, she said to her:

"Go again into the garden, and you will find six lizards behind the watering pot; bring them to me."

She had no sooner done so, but her godmother turned them into six footmen, who skipped up immediately behind the coach, with their liveries all bedaubed with gold and silver, and clung as close behind it, as if they had done nothing else their whole lives. The Fairy then said to Cinderella:

"Well, you see here an equipage fit to go to the ball with; are you not pleased with it?"

"O yes," cried she, "but must I go thither as I am, in these poison nasty

rags?"

Her godmother only just touched her with her wand, and, at the same instant, her clothes were turned into cloth of gold and silver, all beset with jewels. This done she gave her a pair of glass slippers[2], the prettiest in the whole world.

Being thus decked out, she got up into her coach; but her godmother, above all things, commanded her not to stay till after midnight, telling her, at the same time, that if she stayed at the ball one moment longer, her coach would be a pumpkin again, her horses mice, her coachman a rat, her footmen lizards, and her clothes become just as they were before.

She promised her godmother, she would not fail of leaving the ball before midnight; and then away she drove, scarce able to contain herself for joy. The King's son, who was told that a great Princess, whom nobody knew, was come, ran out to receive her; he gave her his hand as she alighted out of the coach, and led her into the hall, among all the company. There was immediately a profound silence, they left off dancing, and the violins ceased to play, so attentive was every one to contemplate the singular beauty of this unknown newcomer. Nothing was then heard but a confused noise of,

"Ha! how handsome she is! Ha! how handsome she is!"

The King himself, old as he was, could not help ogling her, and telling the Queen softly that it was a long time since he had seen so beautiful and lovely a creature. All the ladies were busied in considering her clothes and head-dress, that they might have some made next day after the same pattern, provided they could meet with such fine materials, and as able hands to make them.

The King's son conducted her to the most honourable seat, and afterwards took her out to dance with him: she danced so very gracefully, that they all more and more admired her. A fine collation was served up, whereof the young Prince ate not a morsel, so intently was he busied in gazing on her. She went and sat down by her sisters, showing them a thousand civilities, giving them part of the oranges and citrons which the Prince had presented her with; which very much surprised them, for they did not know her.

While Cinderella was thus amusing her sisters, she heard the clock strike eleven and three quarters, whereupon she immediately made a curtsey to the company, and hasted away as fast as she could.

Being got home, she ran to seek out her godmother, and after having thanked her, she said she could not but heartily wish she might go next day to the ball, because the King's son had desired her. As she was eagerly telling her godmother whatever had passed at the ball, her two sisters knocked at the door which Cinderella ran and opened.

"How long you have stayed," cried she, gaping, rubbing her eyes, and stretching herself as if she had been just awaked out of her sleep; she had not, however, any manner of inclination to sleep since they went from home.

"If thou hadst been at the ball," said one of her sisters, "thou wouldst not have been tired with it; there came thither the finest Princess, the most beautiful ever was seen with mortal eyes; she showed us a thousand civilities, and gave us oranges and citrons." Cinderella was transported with joy; she asked them the name of that Princess; but they told her they did not know it; and that the King's son was very anxious to learn it, and would give all the world to know who she was. At this Cinderella, smiling, replied:

"She must then be very beautiful indeed; Lord! how happy have you been; could not I see her? Ah, dear Miss Charlotte, do lend me your yellow suit of clothes which you wear every day!"

"Ay, to be sure!" cried Miss Charlotte, "lend my clothes to such a dirty Cinder-breech as thou art; who's the fool then?"

Cinderella, indeed, expected some such answer, and was very glad of the refusal; for she would have been sadly put to it, if her sister had lent her what she asked for jestingly.

The next day the two sisters were at the ball, and so was Cinderella, but dressed more magnificently than before. The King's son was always by her, and never ceased his compliments and amorous speeches to her; to whom all this was so far from being tiresome, that she quite forgot what her godmother had recommended to her, so that she, at last, counted the clock striking twelve, when she took it to be no more than eleven; she then rose up, and fled as nimble as a deer.

The Prince followed, but could not overtake her. She left behind one of her glass slippers, which the Prince took up most carefully. She got home, but quite out of breath, without coach or footmen, and in her nasty old clothes, having nothing left her of all her finery, but one of the little slippers, fellow to that she dropped. The guards at the palace gate were asked if they had not seen a Princess go out; who said, they had seen nobody go out, but a young girl, very meanly dressed, and who had more the air of a poor country wench, than a gentlewoman.

When the two sisters returned from the ball, Cinderella asked them if they had been well diverted, and if the fine lady had been there. They told her, Yes, but that she hurried away immediately when it struck twelve, and with so much haste, that she dropped one of her little glass slippers, the prettiest in the world, and which the King's son had taken up; that he had done nothing but look at it during all the latter part of the ball, and that most certainly he was very much in love with the beautiful person who owned the little slipper.

What they said was very true; for a few days after, the King's son caused it to be proclaimed by sound of trumpet, that he would marry her whose foot this slipper would just fit. They whom he employed began to try it on upon the Princesses, then the duchesses, and all the Court, but in vain. It was brought to the two sisters, who did all they possibly could to thrust their feet into the slipper, but they could not effect it.

Cinderella, who saw all this, and knew her slipper, said to them laughing:

"Let me see if it will not fit me?"

Her sisters burst out a-laughing, and began to banter her. The gentleman who was sent to try the slipper, looked earnestly at Cinderella, and finding her very handsome, said it was but just that she should try, and that he had orders to let every one make trial. He invited Cinderella to sit down, and putting the slipper to her foot, he found it went on very easily, and fitted her, as if it had been made of wax. The astonishment her two sisters were in was excessively great, but still abundantly greater, when Cinderella pulled out of her pocket the other slipper, and put it on her foot. Thereupon, in came her godmother, who having touched, with her wand, Cinderella's clothes, made them richer and more magnificent than any of those she had before.

And now her two sisters found her to be that fine beautiful lady whom they had seen at the ball. They threw themselves at her feet, to beg pardon for all the ill treatment they had made her undergo. Cinderella took them up, and as she embraced them, cried that she forgave them with all her heart, and desired them always to love her.

She was conducted to the young Prince, dressed as she was; he thought her more charming than ever, and, a few days after, married her.

Cinderella, who was no less good than beautiful, gave her two sisters lodgings in the palace, and that very same day matched them with two great lords of the court.

[1]'Pinners' were coifs with two long side-flaps pinned on. 'Double-pinners' — with two side-flaps on each side — accurately translates the French *cornettes à deux rangs.*

[2]In Perrault's tale: *pantoufles de verre*. There is no doubt that in the medieval versions of this ancient tale Cinderella was given *pantoufles de vair — i.e.*, of a grey, or grey and white, fur, the exact nature of which has been a matter of controversy, but which was probably a grey squirrel. Long before the seventeenth century the word *vair* had passed out of use, except as a heraldic term, and had ceased to convey any meaning to the people. Thus the *pantoufles de vair* of the fairy tale became, in the oral tradition, the homonymous *pantoufles de verre*, or glass slippers, a delightful improvement on the earlier version.

THE GOLDEN-HEADED FISH

nce upon a time there lived in Egypt a king who lost his sight from a bad illness. Of course he was very unhappy, and became more so as months passed, and all the best doctors in the land were unable to cure him. The poor man grew so thin from misery that everyone thought he was going to die, and the prince, his only son, thought so, too.

Great was, therefore, the rejoicing through Egypt when a traveller arrived in a boat down the river Nile, and after questioning the people as to the reason of their downcast looks, declared that he was court physician to the king of a far country, and would, if allowed, examine the eyes of the blind man. He was at once admitted into the royal presence, and after a few minutes of careful study announced that the case, though very serious, was not quite hopeless.

"Somewhere in the Great Sea," he said, "there exists a Golden-Headed Fish. If you can manage to catch this creature, bring it to me, and I will prepare an ointment from its blood which will restore your sight. For a hundred days I will wait here, but if at the end of that time the fish should still be uncaught, I must return to my own master."

The next morning the young prince set forth in quest of the fish, taking with him a hundred men, each man carrying a net. Quite a little fleet of boats was awaiting them, and in these they sailed to the middle of the Great Sea. During three months they laboured diligently from sunrise to sunset, but though they caught large multitudes of fishes, not one of them had a golden head.

"It is quite useless now," said the prince on the very last night. "Even if we find it this evening, the hundred days will be over in an hour, and long before we could reach the Egyptian capital the doctor will be on his way home. Still, I will go out again, and cast the net once more myself." And so he did, and at the very moment that the hundred days were up, he drew in the net with the Golden-Headed Fish entangled in its meshes.

"Success has come, but, as happens often, it is too late," murmured the young man, who had studied in the schools of philosophy; "but, all the same, put the fish in that vessel full of water, and we will take it back to show my father that we have done what we could." But when he drew near the fish, it looked up at him with such piteous eyes that he could not make up his mind to condemn it to death. For he knew well that, though the doctors of his own country were ignorant of the secret of the ointment, they would do all in their power to extract something from the fish's blood. So he picked up the prize of so much labour, and threw it back into the sea, and then began his journey back to the palace. When at last he reached it, he found the king in a high fever, caused by his disappointment, and he refused to believe the story told him by his son.

"Your head shall pay for it! Your head shall pay for it!" cried he; and bade the courtiers instantly summon the executioner to the palace.

But of course somebody ran at once to the queen, and told her of the king's order, and she put common clothes on the prince, and filled his pockets with gold, and hurried him onboard a ship which was sailing that night for a distant island.

"Your father will repent some day, and then he will be thankful to know you are alive," said she. "But one last counsel will I give you, and that is, take no man into your service who desires to paid every month."

The young prince thought this advice rather odd. If the servant had to be paid anyhow, he did not understand what difference it could make whether it was by the year or by the month. However, he had many times proved that his mother was wiser than he, so he promised obedience.

After a voyage of several weeks, he arrived at the island of which his mother had spoken. It was full of hills and woods and flowers, and beautiful white houses stood everywhere in gardens.

"What a charming spot to live in," thought the prince. And he lost no time in buying one of the prettiest of the dwellings.

Then servants came pressing to offer their services; but as they all declared that they must have payment at the end of every month, the young man, who remembered his mother's words, declined to have anything to say to them. At length, one morning, an Arab appeared and begged that the prince would engage him.

"And what wages do you ask?" inquired the prince, when he had questioned the new-comer and found him suitable.

"I do not want money," answered the Arab; "at the end of a year you can see what my services are worth to you, and can pay me in any way you like." And the young man was pleased, and took the Arab for his servant.

Now, although no one would have guessed it from the look of the side of the island where the prince had landed, the other part was a complete desert, owing to the ravages of a horrible monster which came up from the sea, and devoured all the corn and cattle. The governor had sent bands of soldiers to lie in wait for the creature in order to kill it; but, somehow, no one ever happened to be awake at the moment that the ravages were committed. It was in vain that the sleepy soldiers were always punished severely — the same thing invariably occurred next time; and at last heralds were sent throughout the island to offer a great reward to the man who could slay the monster.

As soon as the Arab heard the news, he went straight to the governor's palace.

"If my master can succeed in killing the monster, what reward will you give him?" asked he.

"My daughter and anything besides that he chooses," answered the governor. But the Arab shook his head.

"Give him your daughter and keep your wealth," said he; "but, henceforward, let her share in your gains, whatever they are."

"It is well," replied the governor; and ordered a deed to be prepared, which was signed by both of them.

That night the Arab stole down to the shore to watch, but, before he set out, he rubbed himself all over with some oil which made his skin smart so badly that there was no chance of *his* going to sleep as the soldiers had done. Then he hid himself behind a large rock and waited. By-and-by a swell seemed to rise on the water, and, a few minutes later, a hideous monster — part bird, part beast, and part serpent — stepped noiselessly on to the rocks.

It walked stealthily up towards the fields, but the Arab was ready for it, and, as it passed, plunged his dagger into the soft part behind the ear. The creature staggered and gave a loud cry, and then rolled over dead, with its feet in the sea.

The Arab watched for a little while, in order to make sure that there was no life left in his enemy, but as the huge body remained quite still, he quitted his hiding-place, and cut off the ears of his foe. These he carried to his master, bidding him show them to the governor, and declare that he himself, and no other, had killed the monster.

"But it was you, and not I, who slew him," objected the prince.

"Never mind; do as I bid you. I have a reason for it," answered the Arab. And though the young man did not like taking credit for what he had never done, at length he gave in.

The governor was so delighted at the news that he begged the prince to take his daughter to wife that very day; but the prince refused, saying that all he desired was a ship which would carry him to see the world. Of course this was granted him at once, and when he and his faithful Arab embarked they found, heaped up in the vessel, stores of diamonds and precious stones, which the grateful governor had secretly placed there.

So they sailed, and they sailed, and they sailed; and at length they reached the shores of a great kingdom. Leaving the prince onboard, the Arab went into the town to find out what sort of a place it was. After some hours he returned, saying that he heard that the king's daughter was the most beautiful princess in the world, and that the prince would do well to ask for her hand.

Nothing loth, the prince listened to this advice, and taking some of the finest necklaces in his hand, he mounted a splendid horse which the Arab had bought for him, and rode up to the palace, closely followed by his faithful attendant.

The strange king happened to be in a good humour, and they were readily admitted to his presence. Laying down his offerings on the steps of the throne, he prayed the king to grant him his daughter in marriage.

The monarch listened to him in silence; but answered, after a pause:

"Young man, I will give you my daughter to wife, if that is your wish; but first I must tell you that she has already gone through the marriage ceremony with a hundred and ninety young men, and not one of them lived for twelve hours after. So think, while there is yet time."

The prince *did* think, and was so frightened that he very nearly went back to his ship without any more words. But just as he was about to withdraw his proposal the Arab whispered:

"Fear nothing, but take her."

"The luck must change some time," he said, at last; "and who would not risk his head for the hand of such a peerless princess?"

"As you will," replied the king. "Then I will give orders that the marriage shall be celebrated to-night."

And so it was done; and after the ceremony the bride and bridegroom retired to their own apartments to sup by themselves, for such was the custom of the country. The moon shone bright, and the prince walked to the window to look out upon the river and upon the distant hills, when his gaze suddenly fell on a silken shroud neatly laid out on a couch, with his name embroidered in gold thread across the front; for this also was the pleasure of the king.

Horrified at the spectacle, he turned his head away, and this time his glance rested on a group of men, digging busily beneath the window. It was a strange hour for anyone to be at work, and what was the hole for? It was a curious shape, so long and narrow, almost like — Ah! yes, that was what it was! It was *his* grave that they were digging!

The shock of the discovery rendered him speechless, yet he stood fascinated and unable to move. At this moment a small black snake darted from the mouth of the princess, who was seated at the table, and wriggled quickly towards him. But the Arab was watching for something of the sort to happen, and seizing the serpent with some pincers that he held in one hand, he cut off its head with a sharp dagger.

The king could hardly believe his eyes when, early the next morning, his new son-in-law craved an audience of his Majesty.

"What, you?" he cried, as the young man entered.

"Yes, I. Why not?" asked the bridegroom, who thought it best to pretend not to know anything that had occurred. "You remember, I told you that the luck must turn at last, and so it has. But I came to ask whether you would be so kind as to bid the gardeners fill up a great hole right underneath my window, which spoils the view."

"Oh! certainly, yes; of course it shall be done!" stammered the king. "Is there anything else?"

"No, nothing, thank you," replied the prince, as he bowed and withdrew.

Now, from the moment that the Arab cut off the snake's head, the spell, or whatever it was, seemed to have been taken off the princess, and she lived very happily with her husband. The days passed swiftly in hunting in the forests, or sailing on the broad river that flowed past the palace, and when night fell she would sing to her harp, or the prince would tell her tales of his own country.

One evening a man in a strange garb, with a face burnt brown by the sun, arrived at court. He asked to see the bridegroom, and falling on his face announced that he was a messenger sent by the Queen of Egypt, proclaiming him king in succession to his father, who was dead.

"Her Majesty begs you will set off without delay, and your bride also, as the affairs of the kingdom are somewhat in disorder," ended the messenger.

Then the young man hastened to seek an audience of his father-in-law, who was delighted to find that his daughter's husband was not merely the governor of a province, as he had supposed, but the king of a powerful country. He at once ordered a splendid ship to be made ready, and in a week's time rode down to the harbour, to bid farewell to the young couple.

In spite of her grief for the dead king, the queen was overjoyed to welcome her son home, and commanded the palace to be hung with splendid stuffs to do honour to the bride. The people expected great things from their new sovereign, for they had suffered much from the harsh rule of the old one, and crowds presented themselves every morning with petitions in their hands, which they hoped to persuade the king to grant. Truly, he had enough to keep him busy; but he was very happy for all that, till, one night, the Arab came to him, and begged permission to return to his own land.

Filled with dismay the young man said: "Leave me! Do you really wish to leave me?" Sadly the Arab bowed his head.

"No, my master; never could I wish to leave you! But I have received a summons, and I dare not disobey it."

The king was silent, trying to choke down the grief he felt at the thought of losing his faithful servant.

"Well, I must not try to keep you," he faltered out at last. "That would be a poor return for all that you have done for me! Everything I have is yours: take what you will, for without you I should long ago have been dead!"

"And without *you*, I should long ago have been dead," answered the Arab. "I am the Golden-Headed Fish."

THE GOLDEN TOUCH

nce upon a time, there lived a very rich man, and a king besides, whose name was Midas; and he had a little daughter, whom nobody but myself ever heard of, and whose name I either never knew, or have entirely forgotten. So, because I love odd names for little girls, I choose to call her Marygold.

This King Midas was fonder of gold than of anything else in the world. He valued his royal crown chiefly because it was composed of that precious metal. If he loved anything better, or half so well, it was the one little maiden who played so merrily around her father's footstool. But the more Midas loved his daughter, the more did he desire and seek for wealth. He thought, foolish man! that the best thing he could possibly do for this dear child would be to bequeath her the immensest pile of yellow, glistening coin, that had ever been heaped together since the world was made. Thus, he gave all his thoughts and all his time to this one purpose. If ever he happened to gaze for an instant at the gold-tinted clouds of sunset, he wished that they were real gold, and that they could be squeezed safely into his strong box. When little Marygold ran to meet him, with a bunch of buttercups and dandelions, he used to say, "Poh, poh, child! If these flowers were as golden as they look, they would be worth the plucking!"

And yet, in his earlier days, before he was so entirely possessed of this insane desire for riches, King Midas had shown a great taste for flowers. He had planted a garden, in which grew the biggest and beautifullest and sweetest roses that any mortal ever saw or smelt. These roses were still growing in the garden, as large, as lovely, and as fragrant as when Midas used to pass whole hours in gazing at them, and inhaling their perfume. But now, if he looked at them at all, it was only to calculate how much the garden would be worth if each of the innumerable rose-petals were a thin plate of gold. And though he once was fond of music (in spite of an idle story about his ears, which were said to resemble those of an ass), the only music for poor Midas, now, was the chink of one coin against another.

At length (as people always grow more and more foolish, unless they take care to grow wiser and wiser), Midas had got to be so exceedingly unreasonable, that he could scarcely bear to see or touch any object that was not gold. He made it his custom, therefore, to pass a large portion of every day in a dark and dreary apartment, under ground, at the basement of his palace. It was here that he kept his wealth. To this dismal hole — for it was little better than a dungeon — Midas betook himself, whenever he wanted to be particularly happy. Here, after carefully locking the door, he would take a bag of gold coin, or a gold cup as big as a washbowl, or a heavy golden bar, or a peck-measure of gold-dust, and bring them from the obscure corners of the room into the one bright and narrow sunbeam that fell from the dungeon-like window. He valued the sunbeam for no other reason but that his treasure would not shine without its help. And then would he reckon over the coins in the bag; toss up the bar, and catch it as it came down; sift the gold-dust through his fingers; look at the funny image of his own face, as reflected in the burnished circumference of the cup; and whisper to himself, "O Midas, rich King Midas, what a happy man art thou!" But it was laughable to see how the image of his face kept grinning at him, out of the polished surface of the cup. It seemed to be aware of his foolish behavior, and to have a naughty inclination to make fun of him.

Midas called himself a happy man, but felt that he was not yet quite so happy as he might be. The very tiptop of enjoyment would never be reached, unless the whole world were to become his treasure-room, and be filled with yellow metal which should be all his own.

Now, I need hardly remind such wise little people as you are, that in the old, old times, when King Midas was alive, a great many things came to pass, which we should consider wonderful if they were to happen in our own day and country. And, on the other hand, a great many things take place nowadays, which seem not only wonderful to us, but at which the people of old times would have stared their eyes out. On the whole, I regard our own times as the strangest of the two; but, however that may be, I must go on with my story.

Midas was enjoying himself in his treasure-room, one day, as usual, when he perceived a shadow fall over the heaps of gold; and, looking suddenly up, what should he behold but the figure of a stranger, standing in the bright and narrow sunbeam! It was a young man, with a cheerful and ruddy face. Whether it was that the imagination of King Midas threw a yellow tinge over everything, or whatever the cause might be, he could not help fancying that the smile with which the stranger regarded him had a kind of golden radiance in it. Certainly, although his figure intercepted the sunshine, there was now a brighter gleam upon all the piled-up treasures than before. Even the remotest corners had their share of it, and were lighted up, when the stranger smiled, as with tips of flame and sparkles of fire.

As Midas knew that he had carefully turned the key in the lock, and that no mortal strength could possibly break into his treasure-room, he, of course, concluded that his visitor must be something more than mortal. It is no matter about telling you who he was. In those days, when the earth was comparatively a new affair, it was supposed to be often the resort of beings endowed with supernatural power, and who used to interest themselves in the joys and sorrows of men, women, and children, half playfully and half seriously. Midas had met such beings before now, and was not sorry to meet one of them again. The stranger's aspect, indeed, was so good-humored and kindly, if not beneficent, that it would have been unreasonable to suspect him of intending any mischief. It was far more probable that he came to do Midas a favor. And what could that favor be, unless to multiply his heaps of treasure?

The stranger gazed about the room; and when his lustrous smile had glistened upon all the golden objects that were there, he turned again to Midas.

"You are a wealthy man, friend Midas!" he observed. "I doubt whether any other four walls, on earth, contain so much gold as you have contrived to pile up in this room."

"I have done pretty well — pretty well," answered Midas, in a discontented tone. "But, after all, it is but a trifle, when you consider that it has taken me my whole life to get it together. If one could live a thousand years, he might have time to grow rich!"

"What!" exclaimed the stranger. "Then you are not satisfied?"

Midas shook his head.

"And pray what would satisfy you?" asked the stranger. "Merely for the curiosity of the thing, I should be glad to know."

Midas paused and meditated. He felt a presentiment that this stranger, with such a golden lustre in his good-humored smile, had come hither with both the power and the purpose of gratifying his utmost wishes. Now, therefore, was the fortunate moment, when he had but to speak, and obtain whatever possible, or seemingly impossible thing, it might come into his head to ask. So he thought, and thought, and thought, and heaped up one golden mountain upon another, in his imagination, without being able to imagine them big enough. At last, a bright idea occurred to King Midas. It seemed really as bright as the glistening metal which he loved so much.

Raising his head, he looked the lustrous stranger in the face.

"Well, Midas," observed the visitor, "I see you have at length hit upon something that will satisfy you. Tell me your wish."

"It is only this," replied Midas. "I am weary of collecting my treasures with so much trouble, and beholding the heap so diminutive, after I have done my best. I wish everything that I touch to be changed to gold!"

The stranger's smile grew so very broad, that it seemed to fill the room like an outburst of the sun, gleaming into a shadowy dell, where the yellow autumnal leaves — for so looked the lumps and particles of gold — lie strewn in the glow of light.

"The Golden Touch!" exclaimed he. "You certainly deserve credit, friend Midas, for striking out so brilliant a conception. But are you quite sure that this will satisfy you?"

"How could it fail?" said Midas.

"And will you never regret the possession of it?"

"What could induce me?" asked Midas. "I ask nothing else to render me perfectly happy."

"Be it as you wish, then," replied the stranger, waving his hand in token of farewell. "To-morrow, at sunrise, you will find yourself gifted with the Golden Touch."

The figure of the stranger then became exceedingly bright, and Midas involuntarily closed his eyes. On opening them again, he beheld only one yellow sunbeam in the room, and, all around him, the glistening of the pre-

cious metal which he had spent his life in hoarding up.

Whether Midas slept as usual that night, the story does not say. Asleep or awake, however, his mind was probably in the state of a child's, to whom a beautiful new plaything has been promised in the morning. At any rate, day had hardly peeped over the hills, when King Midas was broad awake, and, stretching his arms out of bed, began to touch objects that were within reach. He was anxious to prove whether the Golden Touch had really come, according to the stranger's promise. So he laid his finger on a chair by the bedside, and on various other things, but was grievously disappointed to perceive that they remained of exactly the same substance as before. Indeed, he felt very much afraid that he had only dreamed about the lustrous stranger, or else that the latter had been making game of him. And what a miserable affair would it be, if, after all his hopes, Midas must content himself with what little gold he could scrape together by ordinary means, instead of creating it by a touch!

All this while, it was only the gray of the morning, with but a streak of brightness along the edge of the sky, where Midas could not see it. He lay in a very disconsolate mood, regretting the downfall of his hopes, and kept growing sadder and sadder, until the earliest sunbeam shone through the window, and gilded the ceiling over his head. It seemed to Midas that this bright yellow sunbeam was reflected in rather a singular way on the white covering of the bed. Looking more closely, what was his astonishment and delight, when he found that this linen fabric had been transmuted to what seemed a woven texture of the purest and brightest gold! The Golden Touch had come to him with the first sunbeam!

Midas started up, in a kind of joyful frenzy, and ran about the room, grasping at everything that happened to be in his way. He seized one of the bed-posts, and it became immediately a fluted golden pillar. He pulled aside a window-curtain, in order to admit a clear spectacle of the wonders which he was performing; and the tassel grew heavy in his hand — a mass of gold. He took up a book from the table. At his first touch, it assumed the appearance of such a splendidly bound and gilt-edged volume as one often meets with, nowadays; but, on running his fingers through the leaves, behold! it was a bundle of thin golden plates, in which all the wisdom of the book had grown illegible. He hurriedly put on his clothes, and was enraptured to see himself in a magnificent suit of gold cloth, which retained its flexibility and softness, although it burdened him a little with its weight. He drew out his handkerchief, which little Marygold had hemmed for him. That was likewise gold, with the dear child's neat and pretty stitches running all along the border, in gold thread!

Somehow or other, this last transformation did not quite please King Midas. He would rather that his little daughter's handiwork should have remained just the same as when she climbed his knee and put it into his hand.

But it was not worthwhile to vex himself about a trifle. Midas now took his spectacles from his pocket, and put them on his nose, in order that he might see more distinctly what he was about. In those days, spectacles for common people had not been invented, but were already worn by kings; else, how could Midas have had any? To his great perplexity, however, excellent as the glasses were, he discovered that he could not possibly see through them. But this was the most natural thing in the world; for, on taking them off, the transparent crystals turned out to be plates of yellow metal, and, of course, were worthless as spectacles, though valuable as gold. It struck Midas as rather inconvenient that, with all his wealth, he could never again be rich enough to own a pair of serviceable spectacles.

"It is no great matter, nevertheless," said he to himself, very philosophically. "We cannot expect any great good, without its being accompanied with some small inconvenience. The Golden Touch is worth the sacrifice of a pair of spectacles, at least, if not of one's very eyesight. My own eyes will serve for ordinary purposes, and little Marygold will soon be old enough to read to me."

Wise King Midas was so exalted by his good fortune, that the palace seemed not sufficiently spacious to contain him. He therefore went down stairs, and smiled, on observing that the balustrade of the staircase became a bar of burnished gold, as his hand passed over it, in his descent. He lifted the door-latch (it was brass only a moment ago, but golden when his fingers quitted it), and emerged into the garden. Here, as it happened, he found a great number of beautiful roses in full bloom, and others in all the stages of lovely bud and blossom. Very delicious was their fragrance in the morning breeze. Their delicate blush was one of the fairest sights in the world; so gentle, so modest, and so full of sweet tranquillity, did these roses seem to be.

But Midas knew a way to make them far more precious, according to his way of thinking, than roses had ever been before. So he took great pains in going from bush to bush, and exercised his magic touch most indefatigably; until every individual flower and bud, and even the worms at the heart of some of them, were changed to gold. By the time this good work was completed, King Midas was summoned to breakfast; and as the morning air had given him an excellent appetite, he made haste back to the palace.

What was usually a king's breakfast in the days of Midas, I really do not know, and cannot stop now to investigate. To the best of my belief, however, on this particular morning, the breakfast consisted of hot cakes, some nice little brook trout, roasted potatoes, fresh boiled eggs, and coffee, for King Midas himself, and a bowl of bread and milk for his daughter Marygold. At all events, this is a breakfast fit to set before a king; and, whether he had it or not, King Midas could not have had a better.

Little Marygold had not yet made her appearance. Her father ordered her to be called, and, seating himself at table, awaited the child's coming, in order to begin his own breakfast. To do Midas justice, he really loved his daughter, and loved her so much the more this morning, on account of the good fortune which had befallen him. It was not a great while before he heard her coming along the passageway crying bitterly. This circumstance surprised him, because Marygold was one of the cheerfullest little people whom you would see in a summer's day, and hardly shed a thimbleful of tears in a twelvemonth. When Midas heard her sobs, he determined to put little Marygold into better spirits, by an agreeable surprise; so, leaning across the table, he touched his daughter's bowl (which was a China one, with pretty figures all around it), and transmuted it to gleaming gold.

Meanwhile, Marygold slowly and disconsolately opened the door, and showed herself with her apron at her eyes, still sobbing as if her heart would break.

"How now, my little lady!" cried Midas. "Pray what is the matter with you, this bright morning?"

Marygold, without taking the apron from her eyes, held out her hand, in which was one of the roses which Midas had so recently transmuted.

"Beautiful!" exclaimed her father. "And what is there in this magnificent golden rose to make you cry?"

"Ah, dear father!" answered the child, as well as her sobs would let her, "it is not beautiful, but the ugliest flower that ever grew! As soon as I was dressed I ran into the garden to gather some roses for you; because I know you like them, and like them the better when gathered by your little daughter. But, oh dear, dear me! What do you think has happened? Such a misfortune! All the beautiful roses, that smelled so sweetly and had so many lovely blushes, are blighted and spoilt! They are grown quite yellow, as you see this one, and have no longer any fragrance! What can have been the matter with them?"

"Poh, my dear little girl — pray don't cry about it!" said Midas, who was ashamed to confess that he himself had wrought the change which so greatly afflicted her. "Sit down and eat your bread and milk! You will find it easy enough to exchange a golden rose like that (which will last hundreds of years) for an ordinary one which would wither in a day."

"I don't care for such roses as this!" cried Marygold, tossing it contemptuously away. "It has no smell, and the hard petals prick my nose!"

The child now sat down to table, but was so occupied with her grief for the blighted roses that she did not even notice the wonderful transmutation of her China bowl. Perhaps this was all the better; for Marygold was accustomed to take pleasure in looking at the queer figures, and strange trees and houses, that were painted on the circumference of the bowl; and these ornaments were now entirely lost in the yellow hue of the metal.

Midas, meanwhile, had poured out a cup of coffee, and, as a matter of course, the coffee-pot, whatever metal it may have been when he took it up, was gold when he set it down. He thought to himself, that it was rather an extravagant style of splendor, in a king of his simple habits, to breakfast off a service of gold, and began to be puzzled with the difficulty of keeping his treasures safe. The cupboard and the kitchen would no longer be a secure place of deposit for articles so valuable as golden bowls and coffee-pots.

Amid these thoughts, he lifted a spoonful of coffee to his lips, and, sipping it, was astonished to perceive that, the instant his lips touched the liquid, it became molten gold, and, the next moment hardened into a lump!

"Ha!" exclaimed Midas, rather aghast.

"What is the matter, father?" asked little Marygold, gazing at him, with the tears still standing in her eyes.

"Nothing, child, nothing!" said Midas. "Eat your milk, before it gets quite cold."

He took one of the nice little trouts on his plate, and, by way of experiment, touched its tail with his finger. To his horror, it was immediately transmuted from an admirably fried brook trout into a gold-fish, though not one of those gold-fishes which people often keep in glass globes, as ornaments for the parlor. No; but it was really a metallic fish, and looked as if it had been very cunningly made by the nicest goldsmith in the world. Its little bones were now golden wires; its fins and tail were thin plates of gold; and there were the marks of the fork in it, and all the delicate, frothy appearance of a nicely fried fish, exactly imitated in metal. A very pretty piece of work, as you may suppose; only King Midas, just at that moment, would much rather have had a real trout in his dish than this elaborate and valuable imitation of one.

"I don't quite see," thought he to himself, "how I am to get any breakfast!"

He took one of the smoking-hot cakes, and had scarcely broken it, when, to his cruel mortification, though, a moment before, it had been of the whitest wheat, it assumed the yellow hue of Indian meal. To say the truth, if it had really been a hot Indian cake, Midas would have prized it a good deal more than he now did, when its solidity and increased weight made him too bitterly sensible that it was gold. Almost in despair, he helped himself to a boiled egg, which immediately underwent a change similar to those of the trout and the cake. The egg, indeed, might have been mistaken for one of those which the famous goose in the story-book was in the habit of laying; but King Midas was the only goose that had had anything to do with the matter.

"Well, this is a quandary!" thought he, leaning back in his chair, and looking quite enviously at little Marygold, who was now eating her bread and milk with great satisfaction. "Such a costly breakfast before me, and nothing that can be eaten!"

Hoping that, by dint of great dispatch, he might avoid what he now felt to be a considerable inconvenience, King Midas next snatched a hot potato, and attempted to cram it into his mouth, and swallow it in a hurry. But the Golden Touch was too nimble for him. He found his mouth full, not of mealy potato, but of solid metal, which so burnt his tongue that he roared aloud, and, jumping up from the table, began to dance and stamp about the room, both with pain and affright.

"Father, dear father!" cried little Marygold, who was a very affectionate child, "pray what is the matter? Have you burnt your mouth?"

"Ah, dear child," groaned Midas, dolefully, "I don't know what is to become of your poor father!"

And, truly, my dear little folks, did you ever hear of such a pitiable case in all your lives? Here was literally the richest breakfast that could be set before a king, and its very richness made it absolutely good for nothing. The poorest laborer, sitting down to his crust of bread and cup of water, was far better off than King Midas, whose delicate food was really worth its weight in gold. And what was to be done? Already, at breakfast, Midas was excessively hungry. Would he be less so by dinner-time? And how ravenous would be his appetite for supper, which must undoubtedly consist of the same sort of indigestible dishes as those now before him! How many days, think you, would he survive a continuance of this rich fare?

These reflections so troubled King Midas that he began to doubt whether, after all, riches are the one desirable thing in the world, or even the most desirable. But this was only a passing thought. So fascinated was Midas with the glitter of the yellow metal, that he would still have refused to give up the Golden Touch for so paltry a consideration as a breakfast. Just imagine what a price for one meal's victuals! It would have been the same as paying millions and millions of money (and as many millions more as would take forever to reckon up) for some fried trout, an egg, a potato, a hot cake, and a cup of coffee!

"It would be quite too dear," thought Midas.

Nevertheless, so great was his hunger, and the perplexity of his situation, that he again groaned aloud, and very grievously too. Our pretty Marygold could endure it no longer. She sat a moment gazing at her father, and trying, with all the might of her little wits, to find out what was the matter with him. Then, with a sweet and sorrowful impulse to comfort him, she started from her chair, and, running to Midas, threw her arms affectionately about his knees. He bent down and kissed her. He felt that his little daughter's love was worth a thousand times more than he had gained by the Golden Touch.

"My precious, precious Marygold!" cried he.

But Marygold made no answer.

Alas, what had he done? How fatal was the gift which the stranger bestowed! The moment the lips of Midas touched Marygold's forehead, a change had taken place. Her sweet, rosy face, so full of affection as it had been, assumed a glittering yellow color, with yellow tear-drops congealing on her cheeks. Her beautiful brown ringlets took the same tint. Her soft and tender little form grew hard and inflexible within her father's encircling arms. Oh, terrible misfortune! The victim of his insatiable desire for wealth, little Marygold was a human child no longer, but a golden statue!

Yes, there she was, with the questioning look of love, grief, and pity, hardened into her face. It was the prettiest and most woeful sight that ever mortal saw. All the features and tokens of Marygold were there; even the beloved little dimple remained in her golden chin. But, the more perfect was the resemblance, the greater was the father's agony at beholding this golden image, which was all that was left him of a daughter. It had been a favorite phrase of Midas, whenever he felt particularly fond of the child, to say that she was worth her weight in gold. And now the phrase had become literally true. And now, at last, when it was too late, he felt how infinitely a warm and tender heart, that loved him, exceeded in value all the wealth that could be piled up betwixt the earth and sky!

It would be too sad a story, if I were to tell you how Midas, in the fullness of all his gratified desires, began to wring his hands and bemoan himself; and how he could neither bear to look at Marygold, nor yet to look away from her. Except when his eyes were fixed on the image, he could not possibly believe that she was changed to gold. But, stealing another glance, there was the precious little figure, with a yellow tear-drop on its yellow cheek, and a look so piteous and tender, that it seemed as if that very expression must needs soften the gold, and make it flesh again. This, however, could not be. So Midas had only to wring his hands, and to wish that he were the poorest man in the wide world, if the loss of all his wealth might bring back the faintest rose-color to his dear child's face.

While he was in this tumult of despair, he suddenly beheld a stranger standing near the door. Midas bent down his head, without speaking; for he recognized the same figure which had appeared to him the day before in the treasure-room, and had bestowed on him this disastrous faculty of the Golden Touch. The stranger's countenance still wore a smile, which seemed to shed a yellow lustre all about the room, and gleamed on little Marygold's image, and on the other objects that had been transmuted by the touch of

Midas.

"Well, friend Midas," said the stranger, "pray how do you succeed with the Golden Touch?"

Midas shook his head.

"I am very miserable," said he.

"Very miserable, indeed!" exclaimed the stranger. "And how happens that? Have I not faithfully kept my promise with you? Have you not everything that your heart desired?"

"Gold is not everything," answered Midas. "And I have lost all that my heart really cared for."

"Ah! So you have made a discovery, since yesterday?" observed the stranger. "Let us see, then. Which of these two things do you think is really worth the most — the gift of the Golden Touch, or one cup of clear cold water?"

"O blessed water!" exclaimed Midas. "It will never moisten my parched throat again!"

"The Golden Touch," continued the stranger, "or a crust of bread?"

"A piece of bread," answered Midas, "is worth all the gold on earth!"

"The Golden Touch," asked the stranger, "or your own little Marygold, warm, soft, and loving as she was an hour ago?"

"Oh, my child, my dear child!" cried poor Midas, wringing his hands. "I would not have given that one small dimple in her chin for the power of changing this whole big earth into a solid lump of gold!"

"You are wiser than you were, King Midas!" said the stranger, looking seriously at him. "Your own heart, I perceive, has not been entirely changed from flesh to gold. Were it so, your case would indeed be desperate. But you appear to be still capable of understanding that the commonest things, such as lie within everybody's grasp, are more valuable than the riches which so many mortals sigh and struggle after. Tell me now, do you sincerely desire to rid yourself of this Golden Touch?"

"It is hateful to me!" replied Midas.

A fly settled on his nose, but immediately fell to the floor; for it, too, had become gold. Midas shuddered.

"Go, then," said the stranger, "and plunge into the river that glides past the bottom of your garden. Take likewise a vase of the same water and sprinkle it over any object that you may desire to change back again from gold into its former substance. If you do this in earnestness and sincerity, it may possibly repair the mischief which your avarice has occasioned."

King Midas bowed low; and when he lifted his head, the lustrous stranger had vanished.

You will easily believe that Midas lost no time in snatching up a great earthen pitcher (but, alas me! it was no longer earthen after he touched it), and hastening to the river-side. As he scampered along, and forced his way through the shrubbery, it was positively marvelous to see how the foliage turned yellow behind him, as if the autumn had been there, and nowhere else. On reaching the river's brink, he plunged headlong in, without waiting so much as to pull off his shoes.

"Poof! poof! poof!" snorted King Midas, as his head emerged out of the water. "Well; this is really a refreshing bath, and I think it must have quite washed away the Golden Touch. And now for filling my pitcher!"

As he dipped the pitcher into the water, it gladdened his very heart to see it change from gold into the same good, honest earthen vessel which it had been before he touched it. He was conscious, also, of a change within himself. A cold, hard, and heavy weight seemed to have gone out of his bosom. No doubt, his heart had been gradually losing its human substance, and transmuting itself into insensible metal, but had now softened back again into flesh. Perceiving a violet, that grew on the bank of the river, Midas touched it with his finger, and was overjoyed to find that the delicate flower retained its purple hue, instead of undergoing a yellow blight. The curse of the Golden Touch had, therefore, really been removed from him.

King Midas hastened back to the palace; and, I suppose, the servants knew not what to make of it when they saw their royal master so carefully bringing home an earthen pitcher of water. But that water, which was to undo all the mischief that his folly had wrought, was more precious to Midas than an ocean of molten gold could have been. The first thing he did, as you need hardly be told, was to sprinkle it by handfuls over the golden figure of little Marygold.

No sooner did it fall on her than you would have laughed to see how the rosy color came back to the dear child's cheek! and how she began to sneeze and sputter! — and how astonished she was to find herself dripping wet, and her father still throwing more water over her!

"Pray do not, dear father!" cried she. "See how you have wet my nice frock, which I put on only this morning!"

For Marygold did not know that she had been a little golden statue; nor could she remember anything that had happened since the moment when she ran with outstretched arms to comfort poor King Midas.

Her father did not think it necessary to tell his beloved child how very foolish he had been, but contented himself with showing how much wiser he had now grown. For this purpose, he led little Marygold into the garden, where he sprinkled all the remainder of the water over the rosebushes, and with such good effect that above five thousand roses recovered their beautiful bloom. There were two circumstances, however, which, as long as he lived, used to put King Midas in mind of the Golden Touch. One was, that the sands of the river sparkled like gold; the other, that little Marygold's hair had now a golden tinge, which he had never observed in it before she had been transmuted by the effect of his kiss. This change of hue was really an improvement, and made Marygold's hair richer than in her babyhood.

When King Midas had grown quite an old man, and used to trot Marygold's children on his knee, he was fond of telling them this marvelous story, pretty much as I have now told it to you. And then would he stroke their glossy ringlets, and tell them that their hair, likewise, had a rich shade of gold, which they had inherited from their mother.

"And to tell you the truth, my precious little folks," quoth King Midas, diligently trotting the children all the while, "ever since that morning, I have hated the very sight of all other gold, save this!"

JACK AND THE WONDERFUL BEANSTALK

Once upon a time there was a poor widow who lived in a little cottage with her only son Jack. Jack was a giddy, thoughtless boy, but very kindhearted and affectionate. There had been a hard winter, and after it the poor woman had suffered from fever and ague. Jack did no work as yet, and by degrees they grew dreadfully poor. The widow saw that there was no means of keeping Jack and herself from starvation but by selling her cow; so one morning she said to her son:

"I am too weak to go myself, Jack, so you must take the cow to market for me, and sell her."

Jack liked going to market to sell the cow very much; but, as he was on the way, he met a butcher who had some beautiful beans in his hand. Jack stopped to look at them, and the butcher told the boy that they were of great value, and persuaded the silly lad to sell the cow for these beans.

When he brought them home to his mother instead of the money she expected for her nice cow, she was very vexed and shed many tears, scolding Jack for his folly. He was very sorry, and mother and son went to bed very sadly that night; their last hope seemed gone.

At daybreak Jack rose and went out into the garden.

"At least," he thought, "I will sow the wonderful beans. Mother says that they are just common scarlet-runners, and nothing else; but I may as well sow them."

So he took a piece of stick, and made some holes in the ground, and put in the beans.

That day they had very little dinner, and went sadly to bed, knowing that for the next day there would be none and Jack, unable to sleep from grief and vexation, got up at daydawn and went out into the garden.

What was his amazement to find that the beans had grown up in the night, and climbed up and up till they covered the high cliff that sheltered the cottage, and disappeared above it! The stalks had twined and twisted themselves together till they formed quite a ladder.

"It would be easy to climb it," thought Jack.

And, having thought of the experiment, he at once resolved to carry it out, for Jack was a good climber. However, after his late mistake about the cow, he thought he had better consult his mother first.

So Jack called his mother, and they both gazed in silent wonder at the Beanstalk, which was not only of great height, but was thick enough to bear Jack's weight.

"I wonder where it ends," said Jack to his mother; "I think I will climb up and see."

His mother wished him not to venture up this strange ladder, but Jack coaxed her to give her consent to the attempt, for he was certain there must be something wonderful in the Beanstalk. So at last she yielded to his wishes.

Jack instantly began to climb, and went up and up on the ladder-like bean till everything he had left behind him — the cottage, the village, and even the tall church tower — looked quite little, and still he could not see the top of the Beanstalk.

Jack felt a little tired, and thought for a moment that he would go back again; but he was a very persevering boy, and he knew that the way to succeed in anything is not to give up. So after resting for a moment he went on.

After climbing higher and higher, till he grew afraid to look down for fear he should be giddy, Jack at last reached the top of the Beanstalk, and found himself in a beautiful country, finely wooded, with beautiful meadows covered with sheep. A crystal stream ran through the pastures; not far from the place where he had got off the Beanstalk stood a fine, strong castle.

Jack wondered very much that he had never heard of or seen this castle before. But when he reflected on the subject, he saw that it was as much separated from the village by the perpendicular rock on which it stood as if it were in another land.

While Jack was standing looking at the castle, a very strange-looking woman came out of the wood, and advanced towards him.

She wore a pointed cap of quilted red satin turned up with ermine, her hair streamed loose over her shoulders, and she walked with a staff. Jack took off his cap and made her a bow.

"If you please, ma'am," said he, "is this your house?"

"No," said the old lady. "Listen, and I will tell you the story of that castle.

"Once upon a time there was a noble knight, who lived in this castle, which is on the borders of Fairyland. He had a fair and beloved wife and several lovely children. And as his neighbors, the little people, were very friendly towards him, they bestowed on him many excellent and precious gifts.

"Rumor whispered of these treasures; and a monstrous giant, who lived at no great distance, and who was a very wicked being, resolved to obtain possession of them.

"So he bribed a false servant to let him inside the castle, when the knight was in bed and asleep, and he killed him as he lay. Then he went to the part of the castle which was the nursery, and also killed all the poor little ones he found there.

"Happily for her, the lady was not to be found. She had gone with her infant son, who was only two or three months old, to visit her old nurse, who lived in the valley; and she had been detained all night there by a storm.

"The next morning, as soon as it was light, one of the servants at the castle, who had managed to escape, came to tell the poor lady of the sad fate of her husband and her pretty babes. She could scarcely believe him at first, and was eager at once to go back and share the fate of her dear ones. But the old nurse, with many tears, besought her to remember that she had still a child, and that it was her duty to preserve her life for the sake of the poor innocent.

"The lady yielded to this reasoning, and consented to remain at her nurse's house as the best place of concealment; for the servant told her that the giant had vowed, if he could find her, he would kill both her and her baby. Years rolled on. The old nurse died, leaving her cottage and the few articles of furniture it contained to her poor lady, who dwelt in it, working as a peasant for her daily bread. Her spinning-wheel and the milk of a cow, which she had purchased with the little money she had with her, sufficed for the scanty subsistence of herself and her little son. There was a nice little garden attached to the cottage, in which they cultivated peas, beans, and cabbages, and the lady was not ashamed to go out at harvest time, and glean in the fields to supply her little son's wants.

"Jack, that poor lady is your mother. This castle was once your father's, and must again be yours."

Jack uttered a cry of surprise.

"My mother! oh, madam, what ought I to do? My poor father! My dear mother!"

"Your duty requires you to win it back for your mother. But the task is a very difficult one, and full of peril, Jack. Have you the courage to undertake it?"

"I fear nothing when I am doing right," said Jack.

"Then," said the lady in the red cap, "you are one of those who slay giants. You must get into the castle, and if possible possess yourself of a hen that lays golden eggs, and a harp that talks. Remember, all the giant possesses is really yours."

As she ceased speaking, the lady of the red hat suddenly disappeared, and of course Jack knew she was a fairy.

Jack determined at once to attempt the adventure; so he advanced, and blew the horn which hung at the castle portal. The door was opened in a minute or two by a frightful giantess, with one great eye in the middle of her forehead.

As soon as Jack saw her he turned to run away, but she caught him, and dragged him into the castle.

"Ho, ho!" she laughed terribly. "You didn't expect to see *me* here, that is clear! No, I shan't let you go again. I am weary of my life. I am so overworked, and I don't see why I should not have a page as well as other ladies. And you shall be my boy. You shall clean the knives, and black the boots, and make the fires, and help me generally when the giant is out. When he is at home I must hide you, for he has eaten up all my pages hitherto, and you would be a dainty morsel, my little lad."

While she spoke she dragged Jack right into the castle. The poor boy was very much frightened, as I am sure you and I would have been in his place. But he remembered that fear disgraces a man; so he struggled to be brave and make the best of things.

"I am quite ready to help you, and do all I can to serve you, madam," he said, "only I beg you will be good enough to hide me from your husband, for I should not like to be eaten at all."

"That's a good boy," said the Giantess, nodding her head. "It is lucky for you that you did not scream out when you saw me, as the other boys who have been here did, for if you had done so my husband would have awakened and have eaten you, as he did them, for breakfast. Come here, child; go into my wardrobe: he never ventures to open *that*; you will be safe there."

And she opened a huge wardrobe which stood in the great hall, and shut him into it. But the keyhole was so large that it admitted plenty of air, and he could see everything that took place through it. By-and-by he heard a heavy tramp on the stairs, like the lumbering along of a great cannon, and then a voice like thunder cried out:

Fe, fa, fi-fo-fum,
I smell the breath of an Englishman.
Let him be alive or let him be dead,
I'll grind his bones to make my bread.

"Wife," cried the Giant, "there is a man in the castle. Let me have him for breakfast."

"You are grown old and stupid," cried the lady in her loud tones. "It is only a nice fresh steak off an elephant, that I have cooked for you, which you smell. There, sit down and make a good breakfast."

And she placed a huge dish before him of savory steaming meat, which greatly pleased him, and made him forget his idea of an Englishman being in the castle. When he had breakfasted he went out for a walk; and then the Giantess opened the door, and made Jack come out to help her. He helped her all day. She fed him well, and when evening came put him back in the wardrobe.

The Giant came in to supper. Jack watched him through the keyhole, and was amazed to see him pick a wolf's bone, and put half a fowl at a time into his capacious mouth.

When the supper was ended he bade his wife bring him his hen that laid the golden eggs.

"It lays as well as it did when it belonged to that paltry knight," he said. "Indeed I think the eggs are heavier than ever."

The Giantess went away, and soon returned with a little brown hen, which she placed on the table before her husband.

"And now, my dear," she said, "I am going for a walk, if you don't want me any longer."

"Go," said the Giant; "I shall be glad to have a nap by-and-by."

Then he took up the brown hen and said to her:

"Lay!" And she instantly laid a golden egg.

"Lay!" said the Giant again. And she laid another.

"Lay!" he repeated the third time. And again a golden egg lay on the table.

Now Jack was sure this hen was that of which the fairy had spoken. By-and-by the Giant put the hen down on the floor, and soon after went fast asleep, snoring so loud that it sounded like thunder.

Directly Jack perceived that the Giant was fast asleep, he pushed open the door of the wardrobe and crept out; very softly he stole across the room, and, picking up the hen, made haste to quit the apartment. He knew the way to the kitchen, the door of which he found was left ajar. He opened it, shut and locked it after him, and flew back to the Beanstalk, which he descended as fast as his feet would move.

When his mother saw him enter the house she wept for joy, for she had feared that the fairies had carried him away, or that the Giant had found him. But Jack put the brown hen down before her, and told her how he had been in the Giant's castle, and all his adventures. She was very glad to see the hen, which would make them rich once more.

Jack made another journey up the Beanstalk to the Giant's castle one day while his mother had gone to market; but first he dyed his hair and disguised himself. The old woman did not know him again, and dragged him in as she had done before, to help her to do the work; but she heard her husband coming, and hid him in the wardrobe, not thinking that it was the same boy who had stolen the hen. She bade him stay quite still there, or the

Giant would eat him.

Then the Giant came in saying:

> Fe, fa, fi-fo-fum,
> I smell the breath of an Englishman.
> Let him be alive or let him be dead,
> I'll grind his bones to make my bread.

"Nonsense!" said the wife, "it is only a roasted bullock that I thought would be a tit-bit for your supper; sit down and I will bring it up at once."

The Giant sat down, and soon his wife brought up a roasted bullock on a large dish, and they began their supper. Jack was amazed to see them pick the bones of the bullock as if it had been a lark. As soon as they had finished their meal, the Giantess rose and said:

"Now, my dear, with your leave I am going up to my room to finish the story I am reading. If you want me call for me."

"First," answered the Giant, "bring me my money bags, that I may count my golden pieces before I sleep."

The Giantess obeyed. She went and soon returned with two large bags over her shoulders, which she put down by her husband.

"There," she said, " that is all that is left of the knight's money. When you have spent it, you must go and take another baron's castle."

"That he shan't, if I can help it," thought Jack.

The Giant, when his wife was gone, took out heaps and heaps of golden pieces, and counted them, and put them in piles, till he was tired of the amusement. Then he swept them all back into their bags, and leaning back in his chair fell fast asleep, snoring so loud that no other sound was audible.

Jack stole softly out of the wardrobe, and taking up the bags of money, which were his very own, because the Giant had stolen them from his father, he ran off, and with great difficulty descending the Beanstalk, laid the bags of gold on his mother's table. She had just returned from town, and was crying at not finding Jack.

"There, mother, I have brought you the gold that my father lost."

"Oh, Jack, you are a very good boy, but I wish you would not risk your precious life in the Giant's castle. Tell me how you came to go there again."

And Jack told her all about it. Jack's mother was very glad to get the money, but she did not like him to run any risk for her. But after a time Jack

made up his mind to go again to the Giant's castle.

So he climbed the Beanstalk once more, and blew the horn at the Giant's gate. The Giantess soon opened the door; she was very stupid, and did not know him again, but she stopped a minute before she took him in. She feared another robbery; but Jack's fresh face looked so innocent that she could not resist him, and so she bade him come in, and again hid him away in the wardrobe.

By-and-by the Giant came home, and as soon as he had crossed the threshold he roared out:

Fe, fa, fi-fo-fum,
I smell the breath of an Englishman.
Let him be alive or let him be dead,
I'll grind his bones to make my bread.

"You stupid old Giant," said his wife, "you smell only a nice sheep, which I have grilled for your dinner."

And the Giant sat down, and his wife brought up a whole sheep for his dinner. When he had eaten it all up, he said:

"Now bring me my harp, and I will have a little music while you take your walk."

The Giantess obeyed, and returned with a beautiful harp. The framework was all sparkling with diamonds and rubies, and the strings were all of gold.

"This is one of the nicest things I took from the knight," said the Giant. "I am very fond of music, and my harp is a faithful servant."

So he drew the harp towards him, and said:

"Play!"

And the harp played a very soft, sad air.

"Play something merrier!" said the Giant.

And the harp played a merry tune.

"Now play me a lullaby," roared the Giant. And the harp played a sweet lullaby, to the sound of which its master fell asleep.

Then Jack stole softly out of the wardrobe, and went into the huge kitchen to see if the Giantess had gone out. He found no one there, so he went to the door and opened it softly, for he thought he could not do so with the harp in his hand. Then he entered the Giant's room and seized the harp and ran away with it; but as he jumped over the threshold the harp called out:

"Master! Master!"

And the Giant woke up. With a tremendous roar he sprang from his seat, and in two strides had reached the door.

But Jack was very nimble. He fled like lightning with the harp, talking to it as he went (for he saw it was a fairy), and telling it he was the son of its old master, the knight.

Still the Giant came on so fast that he was quite close to poor Jack, and had stretched out his great hand to catch him. But, luckily, just at that moment he stepped upon a loose stone, stumbled, and fell flat on the ground, where he lay at his full length.

This accident gave Jack time to get to the Beanstalk and hasten down it; but just as he reached their own garden he beheld the Giant descending after him.

"Mother! Mother!" cried Jack, "make haste and give me the axe."

His mother ran to him with a hatchet in her hand, and Jack with one tremendous blow cut through all the Beanstalks except one.

"Now, Mother, stand out of the way!" said he.

Jack's mother shrank back, and it was well she did so, for just as the Giant took hold of the last branch of the Beanstalk, Jack cut the stem quite through and darted from the spot. Down came the Giant with a terrible crash, and as he fell on his head, he broke his neck, and lay dead at the feet of the woman he had so much injured. Before Jack and his mother had recovered from their alarm and agitation, a beautiful lady stood before them.

"Jack," said she, "you have acted like a brave knight's son, and deserve to have your inheritance restored to you. Dig a grave and bury the Giant, and then go and kill the Giantess."

"But," said Jack, "I could not kill anyone unless I were fighting with him; and I could not draw my sword upon a woman. Moreover, the Giantess was very kind to me."

The Fairy smiled on Jack.

"I am very much pleased with your generous feeling," she said. "Nevertheless, return to the castle, and act as you will feel needful."

Jack asked the Fairy if she would show him the way to the castle, as the

Beanstalk was now down. She told him that she would drive him there in her chariot, which was drawn by two peacocks. Jack thanked her, and sat down in the chariot with her.

The Fairy drove him a long distance round, till they reached a village which lay at the bottom of the hill. Here they found a number of miserable-looking men assembled. The Fairy stopped her carriage and addressed them:

"My friends," said she, "the cruel giant who oppressed you and ate up all your flocks and herds is dead, and this young gentleman was the means of your being delivered from him, and is the son of your kind old master, the knight."

The men gave a loud cheer at these words, and pressed forward to say that they would serve Jack as faithfully as they had served his father. The Fairy bade them follow her to the castle, and they marched thither in a body, and Jack blew the horn and demanded admittance.

The old Giantess saw them coming from the turret loophole. She was very much frightened, for she guessed that something had happened to her husband; and as she came downstairs very fast she caught her foot in her dress, and fell from the top to the bottom and broke her neck.

When the people outside found that the door was not opened to them, they took crowbars and forced the portal. Nobody was to be seen, but on leaving the hall they found the body of the Giantess at the foot of the stairs.

Thus Jack took possession of the castle. The Fairy went and brought his mother to him, with the hen and the harp. He had the Giantess buried, and endeavored as much as lay in his power to do right to those whom the Giant had robbed. Before her departure for Fairlyland, the Fairy explained to Jack that she had sent the butcher to meet him with the beans, in order to try what sort of lad he was.

"If you had looked at the gigantic Beanstalk and only stupidly wondered about it," she said, "I should have left you where misfortune had placed you, only restoring her cow to your mother. But you showed an inquiring mind, and great courage and enterprise, therefore you deserve to rise; and when you mounted the Beanstalk you climbed the Ladder of Fortune."

She then took her leave of Jack and his mother.

THE HAPPY PRINCE

High above the city, on a tall column, stood the statue of the Happy Prince. He was gilded all over with thin leaves of fine gold, for eyes he had two bright sapphires, and a large red ruby glowed on his sword-hilt.

He was very much admired indeed. "He is as beautiful as a weathercock," remarked one of the Town Councillors who wished to gain a reputation for having artistic tastes; "only not quite so useful," he added, fearing lest people should think him unpractical, which he really was not.

"Why can't you be like the Happy Prince?" asked a sensible mother of her little boy who was crying for the moon. "The Happy Prince never dreams of crying for anything."

"I am glad there is someone in the world who is quite happy," muttered a disappointed man as he gazed at the wonderful statue.

"He looks just like an angel," said the charity children as they came out of the cathedral in their bright scarlet cloaks and their clean white pinafores.

"How do you know?" said the Mathematical Master. "You have never seen one."

"Ah! but we have in our dreams," answered the children; and the Mathematical Master frowned and looked very severe, for he did not approve of children dreaming.

One night there flew over the city a little Swallow. His friends had gone away to Egypt six weeks before, but he had stayed behind, for he was in love with the most beautiful Reed. He had met her early in the spring as he was flying down the river after a big yellow moth, and had been so attracted

by her slender waist that he had stopped to talk to her.

"Shall I love you?" said the Swallow, who liked to come to the point at once, and the Reed made him a low bow. So he flew round and round her, touching the water with his wings, and making silver ripples. This was his courtship, and it lasted all through the summer.

"It is a ridiculous attachment," twittered the other Swallows, "she has no money, and far too many relations"; and indeed the river was quite full of Reeds. Then, when the autumn came, they all flew away.

After they had gone he felt lonely, and began to tire of his lady-love. "She has no conversation," he said, "and I am afraid that she is a coquette, for she is always flirting with the wind." And certainly, whenever the wind blew, the Reed made the most graceful curtsies. "I admit that she is domestic," he continued, "but I love travelling, and my wife, consequently, should love travelling also."

"Will you come away with me?" he said finally to her; but the Reed shook her head, she was so attached to her home.

"You have been trifling with me," he cried; "I am off to the Pyramids. Good-bye!" and he flew away.

All day long he flew, and at night-time he arrived at the city. "Where shall I put up?" he said; "I hope the town has made preparations."

Then he saw the statue on the tall column. "I will put up there," he cried; "it is a fine position with plenty of fresh air." So he alighted just between the feet of the Happy Prince.

"I have a golden bedroom," he said softly to himself as he looked round, and he prepared to go to sleep; but just as he was putting his head under his wing a large drop of water fell on him. "What a curious thing!" he cried; "there is not a single cloud in the sky, the stars are quite clear and bright, and yet it is raining. The climate in the north of Europe is really dreadful. The Reed used to like the rain, but that was merely her selfishness."

Then another drop fell.

"What is the use of a statue if it cannot keep the rain off?" he said. "I must look for a good chimney-pot," and he determined to fly away.

But before he had opened his wings a third drop fell, and he looked up, and saw — Ah! what did he see?

The eyes of the Happy Prince were filled with tears, and tears were running down his golden cheeks. His face was so beautiful in the moonlight that the little Swallow was filled with pity.

"Who are you?" he said.

"I am the Happy Prince."

"Why are you weeping then?" asked the Swallow; "you have quite drenched me."

"When I was alive and had a human heart," answered the statue, "I did not know what tears were, for I lived in the Palace of Sans-Souci, where sorrow is not allowed to enter. In the daytime I played with my companions in the garden, and in the evening I led the dance in the Great Hall. Round the garden ran a very lofty wall, but I never cared to ask what lay beyond it, everything about me was so beautiful. My courtiers called me the Happy Prince, and happy indeed I was, if pleasure be happiness. So I lived, and so I died. And now that I am dead they have set me up here so high that I can see all the ugliness and all the misery of my city, and though my heart is made of lead yet I cannot choose but weep."

"What, is he not solid gold?" said the Swallow to himself. He was too polite to make any personal remarks out loud.

"Far away," continued the statue in a low musical voice, "far away in a little street there is a poor house. One of the windows is open, and through it I can see a woman seated at a table. Her face is thin and worn, and she has coarse, red hands, all pricked by the needle, for she is a seamstress. She is embroidering passion-flowers on a satin gown for the loveliest of the Queen's maids-of-honour to wear at the next Court ball. In a bed in the corner of the room her little boy is lying ill. He has a fever, and is asking for oranges. His mother has nothing to give him but river water, so he is crying. Swallow, Swallow, little Swallow, will you not bring her the ruby out of my sword hilt? My feet are fastened to this pedestal and I cannot move."

"I am waited for in Egypt," said the Swallow. "My friends are flying up and down the Nile, and talking to the large lotus-flowers. Soon they will go to sleep in the tomb of the great King. The King is there himself in his painted coffin. He is wrapped in yellow linen and embalmed with spices. Round his neck is a chain of pale green jade, and his hands are like withered leaves."

"Swallow, Swallow, little Swallow," said the Prince, "will you not stay with me for one night, and be my messenger? The boy is so thirsty and the mother so sad."

"I don't think I like boys," answered the Swallow. "Last summer, when I was staying on the river, there were two rude boys, the miller's sons, who were always throwing stones at me. They never hit me, of course; we swallows fly far too well for that, and, besides, I come of a family famous for its agility; but still, it was a mark of disrespect."

But the Happy Prince looked so sad that the little Swallow was sorry. "It is very cold here," he said; "but I will stay with you for one night, and be your messenger."

"Thank you, little Swallow," said the Prince.

So the Swallow picked out the great ruby from the Prince's sword, and flew away with it in his beak over the roofs of the town.

He passed by the cathedral tower, where the white marble angels were sculptured. He passed by the palace and heard the sound of dancing. A beautiful girl came out on the balcony with her lover. "How wonderful the stars are," he said to her, "and how wonderful is the power of love!" "I hope my dress will be ready in time for the State ball," she answered; "I have ordered passion-flowers to be embroidered on it; but the seamstresses are so lazy."

He passed over the river, and saw the lanterns hanging to the masts of the ships. He passed over the Ghetto, and saw the old Jews bargaining with each other, and weighing out money in copper scales. At last he came to the poor house and looked in. The boy was tossing feverishly on his bed, and the mother had fallen asleep, she was so tired. In he hopped, and laid the great ruby on the table beside the woman's thimble. Then he flew gently round the bed, fanning the boy's forehead with his wings. "How cool I feel," said the boy; "I must be getting better," and he sank into a delicious slumber.

Then the Swallow flew back to the Happy Prince, and told him what he had done. "It is curious," he remarked, "but I feel quite warm now, although it is so cold."

"That is because you have done a good action," said the Prince. And the little Swallow began to think, and then he fell asleep. Thinking always made him sleepy.

When day broke he flew down to the river and had a bath. "What a remarkable phenomenon," said the Professor of Ornithology as he was passing over the bridge. "A swallow in winter!" And he wrote a long letter about it to the local newspaper. Everyone quoted it, it was full of so many words that they could not understand.

"To-night I go to Egypt," said the Swallow, and he was in high spirits at the prospect. He visited all the public monuments, and sat a long time on top of the church steeple. Wherever he went Sparrows chirruped, and said to each other, "What a distinguished stranger!" so he enjoyed himself very much.

When the moon rose he flew back to the Happy Prince. "Have you any commissions for Egypt?" he cried. "I am just starting."

"Swallow, Swallow, little Swallow," said the Prince, "will you not stay with me one night longer?"

"I am waited for in Egypt," answered the Swallow. "To-morrow my friends will fly up to the Second Cataract. The river-horse couches there among the bullrushes, and on a great granite throne sits the God Memnon. All night long he watches the stars, and when the morning star shines, he utters one cry of joy, and then he is silent. At noon the yellow lions come down to the water's edge to drink. They have eyes like green beryls, and their roar is louder than the roar of the cataract."

"Swallow, Swallow, little Swallow," said the Prince, "far away across the city I see a young man in a garret. He is leaning over a desk covered with papers, and in a tumbler by his side there is a bunch of withered violets. His hair is brown and crisp, and his lips are red as a pomegranate, and he has large and dreamy eyes. He is trying to finish a play for the Director of the Theatre, but he is too cold to write any more. There is no fire in the grate, and hunger has made him faint."

"I will wait with you one night longer," said the Swallow, who really had a good heart. "Shall I take him another ruby?"

"Alas! I have no ruby now," said the Prince; "my eyes are all that I have left. They are made of rare sapphires, which were brought out of India a thousand years ago. Pluck out one of them and take it to him. He will sell it to the jeweller, and buy food and firewood, and finish his play."

"Dear Prince," said the Swallow, "I cannot do that;" and he began to weep.

"Swallow, Swallow, little Swallow," said the Prince, "do as I command you."

So the Swallow plucked out the Prince's eye, and flew away to the student's garret. It was easy enough to get in, as there was a hole in the roof. Through this he darted, and came into the room. The young man had his head buried in his hands, so he did not hear the flutter of the bird's wings, and when he looked up he found the beautiful sapphire lying on the withered violets.

"I am beginning to be appreciated," he cried; "this is from some great admirer. Now I can finish my play," and he looked quite happy.

The next day the Swallow flew down to the harbour. He sat on the mast of a large vessel and watched the sailors hauling big chests out of the hold with ropes. "Heave ahoy!" they shouted as each chest came up. "I am going to Egypt!" cried the Swallow, but nobody minded, and when the moon rose he flew back to the Happy Prince.

"I am come to bid you good-bye," he cried.

"Swallow, Swallow, little Swallow," said the Prince, "will you not stay with me one night longer?"

"It is winter," answered the Swallow, "and the chill snow will soon be here. In Egypt the sun is warm on the green palm-trees, and the crocodiles lie in the mud and look lazily about them. My companions are building a nest in the Temple of Baalbek, and the pink and white doves are watching them, and cooing to each other. Dear Prince, I must leave you, but I will never forget you, and next spring I will bring you back two beautiful jewels in place of those you have given away. The ruby shall be redder than a red rose, and the sapphire shall be as blue as the great sea."

"In the square below," said the Happy Prince, "there stands a little match-girl. She has let her matches fall in the gutter, and they are all spoiled. Her father will beat her if she does not bring home some money, and she is crying. She has no shoes or stockings, and her little head is bare. Pluck out my other eye, and give it to her, and her father will not beat her."

"I will stay with you one night longer," said the Swallow, "but I cannot pluck out your eye. You would be quite blind then."

"Swallow, Swallow, little Swallow," said the Prince, "do as I command you."

So he plucked out the Prince's other eye and darted down with it. He swooped past the match-girl, and slipped the jewel into the palm of her hand. "What a lovely bit of glass," cried the little girl; and she ran home laughing.

Then the Swallow came back to the Prince, "You are blind now," he said, "so I will stay with you always."

"No, little Swallow," said the poor Prince. "you must go away to Egypt."

"I will stay with you always," said the Swallow, and he slept at the Prince's feet.

All the next day he sat on the Prince's shoulder, and told him stories of what he had seen in strange lands. He told him of the red ibises, who stand in long rows on the banks of the Nile and catch gold-fish in their beaks; of the Sphinx, who is as old as the world itself, and lives in the desert, and knows everything; of the merchants, who walk slowly by the side of their camels, and carry amber beads in their hands; of the King of the Mountains of the Moon, who is as black as ebony, and worships a large crystal; of the great green snake that sleeps in a palm-tree, and has twenty priests to feed it with honey-cakes, and of the pygmies who sail over a big lake on large flat leaves, and are always at war with the butterflies.

"Dear little Swallow," said the Prince, "you tell me of marvelous things, but more marvelous than anything is the suffering of men and of women. There is no Mystery so great as Misery. Fly over my city, little Swallow, and tell me what you see there."

So the Swallow flew over the great city, and saw the rich making merry in their beautiful houses, while the beggars were sitting at the gates. He flew into dark lanes, and saw the white faces of starving children looking out listlessly at the black streets. Under the archway of a bridge two little boys were lying in one another's arms to try to keep themselves warm. "How hungry we are!" they said. "You must not lie here," shouted the watchman, and they wandered out into the rain.

Then he flew back and told the Prince what he had seen.

"I am covered with fine gold," said the Prince; "you must take it off leaf by leaf, and give it to my poor; the living always think that gold can make them happy."

Leaf after leaf of the fine gold the Swallow picked off, till the Happy Prince looked quite dull and grey. Leaf after leaf of the fine gold he brought to the poor, and the children's faces grew rosier, and they laughed and played games in the street. "We have bread now!" they cried.

Then the snow came, and after the snow came the frost. The streets looked as if they were made of silver, they were so bright and glistening;

long icicles like crystal daggers hung down from the eaves of the houses, everybody went about in furs, and the little boys wore scarlet caps and skated on the ice.

The poor little Swallow grew colder and colder, but he would not leave the Prince; he loved him too well. He picked up crumbs outside the baker's door when the baker was not looking, and tried to keep himself warm by flapping his wings.

But at last he knew that he was going to die. He had just enough strength to fly up to the Prince's shoulder once more. "Good-bye, dear Prince!" he murmured. "Will you let me kiss your hand?"

"I am glad that your are going to Egypt at last, little Swallow," said the Prince, "you have stayed too long here; but you must kiss me on the lips, for I love you?"

"It is not to Egypt that I am going," said the Swallow. "I am going to the House of Death. Death is the brother of Sleep, is he not?"

And he kissed the Happy Prince on the lips, and fell down dead at his feet.

At that moment a curious crack sounded inside the statue as if something had broken. The fact is that the leaden heart had snapped right in two. It certainly was a dreadfully hard frost.

Early the next morning the Mayor was walking in the square below in company with the Town Councillors. As they passed the column he looked up at the statue. "Dear me! how shabby the Happy Prince looks!" he said.

"How shabby indeed!" cried the Town Councillors, who always agreed with the Mayor, and they went up to look at it.

"The ruby has fallen out of his sword, his eyes are gone, and he is golden no longer," said the Mayor; "in fact, he is little better than a beggar!"

"Little better than a beggar," said the Town Councillors.

"And here is actually a dead bird at his feet!" continued the Mayor. "We must really issue a proclamation that birds are not to be allowed to die here." And the Town Clerk made a note of the suggestion.

So they pulled down the statue of the Happy Prince. "As he is no longer beautiful he is no longer useful," said the Art Professor at the University.

Then they melted the statue in a furnace, and the Mayor held a meeting of the Corporation to decide what was to be done with the metal. "We must

have another statue, of course," he said, "and it shall be a statue of myself."

"Of myself," said each of the Town Councillors, and they quarrelled. When I last heard of them they were quarrelling still.

"What a strange thing!" said the overseer of the workmen at the foundry. "This broken lead heart will not melt in the furnace. We must throw it away." So they threw it on a dust-heap where the the dead Swallow was also lying.

"Bring me the two most precious things in the city," said God to one of His angels; and the Angel brought Him the leaden heart and the dead bird.

"You have rightly chosen," said God, "for in my garden of Paradise this little bird shall sing forevermore, and in my city of gold the Happy Prince shall praise me."

THE ONE-FOOTED FAIRY

There was once a fairy who sat down while the others were dancing. His name was Tippitin, and he was a very happy fairy, though he never seemed to know any of the things the other fairies knew. Some fairies know how to paint flowers, and they always do it by night when nobody is looking. One has a tube of blue paint, and he squeezes it on the larkspurs, and another has a tube of red paint, and he splashes it over the roses. The cleverest ones of all know how to paint spots on the tiger-lilies and streaks on the sweet-williams; and the very clever ones indeed can touch up a pansy's face so that you would hardly think it was painted at all. You'd say it just grew so. These clever ones that have the streaky-spotty work to do often use little brushes made out of the fur of a cat's tail. One hair is enough for a fine brush, and two at the most for a very heavy one; but the cats hate to have them pulled out. The fairies are very cautious about doing it when no one knows: so they always take the time when a cat is crying for something else. If a cat gets her foot stepped on, or even if she is just waiting outside the door to be let in, and cries to mention it, a dozen or two fairies are always waiting to pounce on her and pull out as many tail-hairs as they can before the *meow* is finished. So that, although you can't see them, you may be very sure every cat is followed by at least two dozen fairy merchants, waiting to pull hairs from her tail and sell them to the fairy painters. I forgot to say that only the hairs from the tails of red and pink cats will do at all: so it would be of no use to make everyday cats cry, to help the fairies. Only the red and pink ones will do. But Tippitin did not know how to paint flowers.

Then some fairies know how to make round, clear drops that you can see through. They make them out of icicles. But Tippitin did not know that.

Some fairies know how to make beautiful bicycle wheels out of nice round spiders' webs when they find them. But Tippitin did not know that.

Some fairies can sweep up the kitchen for you, if they like you, or make the butter come very fast, or keep it from coming at all. But Tippitin did not know how to do that. He only knew how to dance; and one night when all the other fairies in that province of the kingdom were dancing, he did not dance at all. He just sat down on a pebble and drew a big leaf up over his knees. The fairies were dancing very hard that night, because they were practicing for a big Circle Dance that would be held the next night, which was the night of the full moon. And the Queen was coming. She had been in Lapland for seven nights — which is a very long time when you are a fairy — and she was coming back to tell her people what she saw. She really went up there to see if the patterns of snow-crystals were any different from the patterns all over the rest of the world, and if they were, to bring some home. The fairies were wild to know that. Some fairies can freeze snow-crystals. But Tippitin couldn't do that.

Now when they were dancing, they found there was a gap in the ring, and they all stopped short. They knew at once how it was. Some fairy was not there.

"Why, it's Tippitin!" said one; and as this was the night when they all said things together — it is the night before the night of the full moon — they all cried: "Why, it's Tippitin!"

"Tippitin, where are you?" called one; and then the others all called: "Tippitin, where are you?"

Tippitin only drew up the leaf a little higher over his knees.

"Oh," said he gruffly, "I'm here. Don't you see me?"

"He's here," said all the fairies. "Don't we see him?"

They crowded up about him, and climbed on the leaves over his head and looked down at him; but Tippitin only tucked the leaf in round his knees.

"Why don't you dance with us, Tippitin?" they asked him.

Tippitin put out his lips, as if he felt very big, and drew his shoulders up to his ears, as if he needn't answer at all if he didn't want to.

"Oh," said he, "I'm not dancing to-night."

"Oh," said the fairies, "he's not dancing to-night!"

Then they looked at one another and wondered what they could say next, for it is very serious for a fairy to say he won't dance. It is exactly as if a boy or a girl should say, "I won't learn two times two, or 'Catch'!" But they were all thinking the same thing, and in a minute they all said it.

"But, Tippitin, you'll have to dance. For this is the new Circle Dance, and if you don't learn it to-night you won't know it, and if you don't know it you can't dance it to-morrow night when the Queen is here, and what will you do then, Tippitin?"

"Nothing," said Tippitin.

The fairies looked at one another, and their eyes grew very large, and their mouths grew round.

"Nothing!" they all said. "Tippitin will do nothing. That is what Tippitin will do — nothing!"

Tippitin twisted up his face and squirmed about on the pebble.

"You go away," said he, "and let me alone. I shan't dance to-night, and I shan't dance to-morrow night."

"But what will the Queen say?" they all cried.

"I don't know," said Tippitin.

Then they all looked at one another and said: "He doesn't know." And they were silent for a very long time.

But after the very long time was over, they suddenly thought they must go and look at the Queen's throne and see if it was all right and tight for her to use. Now a great many things will do for a queen's throne — a tuft of moss or an opening rose or a clover head — oh, there are a great many things! But in this particular province there was one tiny piece of bark the Queen had taken a great liking to, for a throne. The little borers-in-the-wood had carved it beautifully for her, so that it was of a wonderful pattern; and it had fallen from the tree in exactly the right position, so that it was tilted up a little for a back, and tilted sidewise a little for the arms. The Queen had said she never saw anywhere such a comfortable throne, and she believed she should find it so if she lived to be ten million and ten. And then the fairies all laughed until the owls brought their two yellow lanterns to see what was the matter, for everybody knows fairies never live to be ten million and ten. They only live Forever. That was a great joke of the Queen's, and it was repeated everywhere all over the kingdom, and is being repeated now — or it will be to-night, if the moon is full.

Now somebody had discovered, not long before this night when they were making ready for the Queen, that her throne seemed a little unsteady. A rabbit running through the wood may have joggled it, or some mortal, walking that way, may have hit it with his foot, not knowing how important it was to let it alone. And really it is surprising that mortals know so very little about what is against the law in the woods. There are ever so many things you can do if you stop and take off your cap and say, "By your leave," or even make a bow. But there is one thing that must never be done. Things that are good wood-citizens, like lady's-slipper, or fern, or anything that blooms red, pink, blue, white, or yellow, must never be pulled up by the roots. Sometimes you may take them up very carefully and carry them to live somewhere else; but you must be perfectly sure you know beforehand that you are going to put them in the same kind of place they are used to living in, and that they are going to get water enough to drink. There are very dreadful punishments for people who pull up things that bloom red, or pink, or blue, or white, or yellow, and throw them down and leave them to die. I will not tell you what the punishment is. If you want to find out, you can look in the Fairy Code.

But to-night, when the fairies went to look at the Queen's throne, they found it was as firm and solid as a throne could be. They pushed at it, and pulled at it — of course they dared not sit in it — and they all breathed a great breath and said, "Well, that's all right," and they trooped away and began dancing again. But Tippitin still sat with the leaf over his knees, and he would not dance.

The next night, at exactly twelve o'clock, the owls began to call, "Who? Who?" and the fairies all answered, "Her Majesty! Her most lovely-dear-and-glorious-splendid Majesty, the Queen!"

And then all the woods waked up, and even the little grasshopper and cricket things in fields beyond the woods, got out their musical instruments and piped and piped, and the farmhouse dog called out, "Something's up! Hark! Hark!" But as he said it, he went into his kennel, just as far as he could, and sat there with his tail tucked under him; for every dog knows what is going on in the woods at night and that he'd better say as little about it as possible.

The Queen had come straight through from Lapland by the Crystal

Express, and her chariot had not yet melted. It was the most beautiful carved ice you ever saw, and the canopy over it was the loveliest spun frost. It was drawn by six Northern Lights; but they had to be unharnessed at once, so that they could go back, because they were needed to make an illumination for a Labor Night parade of the Frosts and Snows. The Queen had hired them on that condition. So when they unharnessed themselves and flashed off, she nodded at them very kindly, and then she turned to her own people and told them to stand where they were and see her chariot melt. It was a little surprise she had arranged for them, because it is very unusual to see an ice-chariot in the woods on a warm summer night. This night was very warm indeed, and the chariot melted fast; but quickly as it went, a great many fairy artists stood by to draw the forms of the snow-crystals, to see if they could copy them next winter, and they really got a great many ideas.

And when the chariot and the canopy were quite gone, and there was only a tiny puddle of water left where they had been, the Queen turned to her subjects and said: "Now, to the dance!"

So they joined hands and made a circle about the Queen, and danced their new dance. And Tippitin sat in a dark little corner under a leaf, and did not dance at all. He had taken a thick shadow and wrapped it about him, and if you had been there, even if you could have seen the others, you could not have seen him. Of course the Queen could have seen him, if she had looked, because fairy eyes are the best in the woods, and the Queen's eyes are the very best; but she was watching the new dance to decide how she liked it, and though there was still the gap in the circle where Tippitin ought to have been, the fairies made other gaps, from time to time, so that she should think they were a part of the dance. For they all loved Tippitin, and they were afraid she would blame him. When the dance was over and the Queen had said it was very nice indeed, though not the nicest ever, they looked at one another and shut their mouths tight because they did not dare to speak.

"It's a nice dance," said the Queen again.

"It's a welcoming dance, your most lovely-dear-and-glorious-splendid Majesty," said all the fairies together, trembling. (They were not afraid for themselves, because the Queen is kinder than you could ever think, and no fairy fears her without reason, and just because she is a queen. But they

were afraid for Tippitin.)

"That is what it is called — the Welcoming Dance."

The Queen put her hand to her chin and meditated. She had caught that trick from the Ice-King in the North, who had a beard.

"It's a nice dance," she said, "but I miss something in it. I don't know quite what it is, but it's something very fast and sure, and always coming down in the right place. Just take me to my throne. I shall be able to think better there."

So the fairies formed themselves into a guard in front and a following behind, and they took her to her throne. They were very silent all the way, because they knew they were leaving Tippitin sitting wrapped in his thick shadow behind, and of course they knew, too, just what the Queen missed in the dance. It was Tippitin.

But when the Queen had seated herself on her throne, they began to smile again, for she leaned back against the carven wood and sighed a peaceful, happy sigh, and said: "Now I am at home again. This old throne is worth a million crystal palaces." (You see if you are a queen you always think in millions. One palace is altogether too few to talk about.) "Now," said the Queen, "we'll have the dance again."

So the fairies formed themselves before her into the circle with the gap in it, and they danced and they danced, and all the more gayly because they didn't want her to find out anything was the matter.

But presently the Queen cried out: "Stop! Stop!"

And they had to stop, and the circle with the gap in it was broken, and there were more than forty gaps.

"I should like to be told," said the Queen, rather grandly, "what is the matter with this throne!"

The fairies all trembled.

"Your Majesty," they said, "your most lovely-dear-and-glorious-splendid Majesty," said they, "it is your own favorite throne."

"So I thought," said the Queen. "But there's something under it."

"Something under it!" cried all the fairies. "What is it that is under it, your most lovely-dear-and-glorious-splendid Majesty?"

"That is what I should like to be told," said the Queen. "It's something that wants to dance: for when you were dancing, it kept knocking under my throne, and when you stopped, it stopped, too. Lift up the throne and see."

So the fairies crowded round the throne and tugged at it with all their might; but they could not lift it. Of course it would do no good to try to overturn it, because a fairy throne is the one thing you can never overturn.

"Well," said the Queen, putting her hand to her chin, "try the dance again, and we'll see!"

So they formed their circle with the gap in it, and this time the Queen began to sing: —

Around and about!
What is hidden, come out
What is veiled must be seen
'T is the will of the Queen!

And the throne began to tremble, and it settled a little to one side, for there danced out of it the tiniest foot you ever saw, and danced into the gap in the circle, and danced and danced.

"Aha!" cried the Queen. "Now the dance is almost the nicest dance that ever was, but not quite."

Slow little foot, slow! slow!
Go little foot, go! go!
Follow, fairies, follow me
And we'll see, we'll see, we'll see.

And the fairies stopped dancing, and the little foot stopped too, and it began to hop through the woods so fast it was like the drop-drop-drop of water off a leaf after a shower, and the Queen and the fairies followed it. And what did the foot do but hop straight up to Tippitin, sitting wrapped in his shadow; and when Tippitin saw it, he cried out very loud, and threw off the shadow, and the Queen and all the fairies saw he had but one foot. And the little foot hopped up to Tippitin's ankle, and Tippitin bent down and screwed it on, and there he stood on his two trim feet, and made the Queen a beautiful low bow.

"Why, Tippitin!" said the Queen. "Why, Tippitin, what made you take your foot off?"

"Your Majesty," said Tippitin, "I went to look at your Majesty's throne one day to see if it was all right and tight, and I found there was a little hollow under it, and it made your Majesty's throne jiggle. And I couldn't find

anything that exactly fitted, to fill up the hollow, and my foot fitted, so I just rammed it in there, — that's all"

The Queen and the fairies looked at him for as much as seven minutes, and they were all deeply affected. Then the Queen spoke.

"Henceforth," said she, "I appoint Tippitin to be the very-much-to-be-honored keeper of my wood-bark throne. And if he finds cause to think it needs repair, he may call upon all the clever workmen of my kingdom to set it right again. But his own feet are needed for my service in the dancing that keeps my kingdom standing while mortal thrones go down. Now, fairies, to the dance!"

And the fairies formed a circle with no gap in it, because Tippitin was there, and they danced the dance as it was first intended to be, with no gaps in it, and when it was over, the Queen clapped her hands and said: "Now I see what I missed out of the dance. It was Tippitin! And now it is the most perfectly lovely dance that ever was!"

THUMBELINA

nce upon a time there was a woman who wished very much to have a very small child, but she did not know where to get one. So she went to an old witch and said to her: "I would so very much like to have a small child; can you tell me where I can get one?"

"Oh, we shall soon be able to manage that," said the witch. "Here is a barleycorn; it is not of the same kind that grows in the farmer's field, or that the chickens get to eat. Put it into a flower-pot, and you will see something."

"Thank you," said the woman, and gave the witch twelve shillings, for that was the price of it. Then she went home and planted the barleycorn; immediately there grew up a large handsome flower, looking like a tulip; the leaves, however, were tightly closed, as though it were still a bud. "It is a beautiful flower," said the woman, kissing its red and yellow leaves; but as she kissed it, the flower opened with a bang. It was a real tulip, as could now be seen; but in the middle of the flower, on the green velvety pistils, sat a tiny maiden, delicately and gracefully formed. She was scarcely half a thumb's length high, and therefore she was called Thumbelina.

A neat, polished walnut-shell served Thumbelina for a cradle, blue violet leaves were her mattresses, and a rose-leaf her blanket. There she slept at night, but in the daytime she played about on the table, where the woman had put a plate with a wreath of flowers round it, the stalks of which stood in water. On this water floated a large tulip leaf, and on this she could sit and row from one side of the plate to the other, having two white horse-hairs for oars. It looked wonderfully pretty. She could sing, too, and indeed, so tenderly and prettily as had never been heard before.

One night, as she was lying in her pretty bed, an old toad came creeping in through the window, in which there was a broken pane. The toad was a very ugly one, large and wet; it hopped down upon the table, where Thumbelina lay sleeping under the red rose-leaf.

"She would be a pretty wife for my son," said the toad, taking the walnut-shell in which Thumbelina was sleeping, and hopping with it through the window, down into the garden.

There flowed a great wide brook, the margin of which was swampy and marshy, and here lived the toad with her son. Ugh! he was so ugly and nasty, and looked just like his mother. "Croak, croak! Crek-kek-kex!" was all that he could say when he spied the graceful little girl in the walnut shell.

"Don't speak so loud, else you'll wake her," said the old toad. "She might run away from us, for she is as light as swan's-down, so we will put her on one of the broad leaves of the water-lily in the brook; that will be just like an island for her, she is so light and small. She will not be able to run away from there while we are getting ready the state-room under the marsh, where you are to live and keep house."

Out in the brook there grew a great many water-lilies with broad green leaves, which looked as though they were floating on the water; the leaf which lay farthest off was the largest, to this the old toad swam out, and laid the walnut-shell with Thumbelina upon it.

Tiny Thumbelina woke early in the morning, and when she saw where she was she began to cry very bitterly; for there was water on every side of the great green leaf, and she could not get to land.

The old toad was sitting in the marsh decking out her room with reeds and yellow flowers — it was to be made very pretty for the new daughter-in-law; then she swam out with her ugly son to the leaf where Thumbelina was. They wanted to fetch her pretty bed, which was to be placed in the bridal chamber before she herself entered it. The old toad bowed low in the water before her and said: "Here you have my son; he will be your husband, and you will live in great splendor down in the marsh."

"Croak, croak! Crek-kek-kex!" was all that the son could say. Then they took the pretty little bed and swam away with it, leaving Thumbelina sitting alone on the green leaf, crying, for she did not want to live with the nasty old toad, or have her ugly son for a husband. The little fishes swimming

down in the water had both seen the toad and also heard what she had said; so they put out their heads, for they wanted to see the little girl too. As soon as they saw her, they thought her so pretty that they felt very sorry that she was to go down to the ugly toad. No, that should never be! They assembled together down in the water, round the green stalk that held the leaf on which the tiny maiden stood, and with their teeth they gnawed away the stalk; the leaf floated away down the stream with Thumbelina — far away, where the toad could not reach her.

Thumbelina sailed by many towns, and the little birds sitting in the bushes saw her and sang, "What a lovely little girl!" The leaf went floating away with her farther and farther, and so Thumbelina travelled right out of the country.

A pretty little white butterfly kept fluttering around her, and at last sat down upon the leaf. Thumbelina pleased him, and she was very glad of it, for now the toad could not reach her, and it was so beautiful where she was; the sun was shining on the water, making it sparkle like the brightest silver. She took her girdle, and tied one end of it round the butterfly, fastening the other end of the ribbon to the leaf; it glided along much quicker now, and she too, for of course she was standing on it.

A great cockchafer came flying along, who spied her, and immediately clasped his claws round her slender waist and flew up with her into a tree. The green leaf floated down the stream, and the butterfly with it; for he was bound fast to the leaf and could not get away.

Heavens! how frightened poor Thumbelina was when the cockchafer flew up into the tree with her. But she was mostly grieved for the sake of the beautiful white butterfly which she had bound fast; in case he could not free himself, he would be obliged to starve. But the cockchafer did not care about that. He sat down with her on the largest green leaf of the tree, gave her the honey from the flowers to eat, and told her that she was very pretty, although she was not at all like a cockchafer.

Later on all the other cockchafers who lived in the tree came to pay a visit; they looked at Thumbelina and said, "She has not even more than two legs; that looks miserable!" "She hasn't any feelers," said another. "She has such a narrow waist, and looks quite human. Ugh, how ugly she is!" said all the lady cockchafers; and yet Thumbelina was very pretty — even the cockchafer who had carried her off admitted that. But when all the others said she was ugly, he at last believed it too, and would no longer have her; she might go where she liked. So they flew from off the tree with her and put her upon a daisy; she wept because she was so ugly that the cockchafers would not have her, and yet she was the loveliest little girl that one could imagine — as delicate and as tender as the most beautiful rose-leaf.

The whole summer through poor Thumbelina lived alone in the great forest. She wove herself a bed out of blades of grass, and hung it under a shamrock, in order to be protected from the rain; she gathered the honey out of the flowers for food, and drank of the dew that was on the leaves every morning. In this way summer and autumn passed, but now came winter — the long, cold winter. All the birds who had sung so beautifully about her flew away; the trees became bare and the flowers faded. The large shamrock under which she had lived dried up, and there remained nothing of it but a withered stalk; she was dreadfully cold, for her clothes were in tatters, and she herself was so small and delicate. Poor little Thumbelina, she would be frozen to death. It began to snow, and every snow-flake that fell upon her was like a whole shovelful thrown upon us; for we are so tall, and she was only an inch long. So she wrapped herself in a dry leaf, but that tore in half and would not warm her; she was shivering with cold.

Close to the wood to which she had now come lay a large cornfield; but the corn was gone long since, and only the dry naked stubbles stood up out of the frozen ground. These were like a forest for her to wander through, and oh! how she was trembling with cold. In this state she reached the door of a field-mouse who occupied a hole under the corn stubbles. There the mouse lived comfortably, had a whole room full of corn, a splendid kitchen and larder. Poor Thumbelina stood before the door like a little beggar girl, and asked for a piece of a barley-corn, for she had not had a bit to eat for two days.

"You poor little creature!" said the field-mouse — for she was really a good old mouse — "come into my warm room and dine with me."

Now, being pleased with Thumbelina, she said: "If you like, you can stay with me the whole winter, but you must keep my room clean and neat, and tell me tales, for I am very fond of them." And Thumbelina did what the good old field-mouse wished, and in return was treated uncommonly well.

"Now we shall soon have a visit," said the field-mouse; "my neighbor is in the habit of visiting me once a week. He is even better off than I am; has large rooms, and wears a beautiful black velvety fur. If you could only get him for a husband you would be well provided for. But he cannot see. You must tell him the prettiest stories that you know."

But Thumbelina did not trouble herself about it: she did not think much of the neighbor, for he was only a mole.

He came and paid a visit in his black velvety fur. He was so rich and so learned, said the field-mouse, and his dwelling was twenty times larger than hers; he possessed great learning, but he could not bear the sun and the beautiful flowers. Of the latter he seldom spoke, for he had never seen them.

Thumbelina had to sing, and she sang: "Cockchafer, cockchafer, fly away." and "When the parson goes afield." So the mole fell in love with her because of her beautiful voice; but he said nothing, for he was a prudent man.

A short time before, he had dug a passage through the earth from his house to theirs, and the field-mouse and Thumbelina received permission to take a walk in this passage as often as they liked. But he begged them not to be afraid of the dead bird which lay there. It was an entire bird, with feathers and beak, who had probably died only a short time before, and was buried just where the mole had made his passage.

The mole took a piece of decayed wood in his mouth, for that glimmers like a light in the dark, and then went on in front, and lighted them through the long dark passage. When they came to the spot where the dead bird lay, the mole thrust his broad nose against the ceiling and pushed the earth up, so that a large hole was made, through which the light could shine down. In the middle of the floor lay a dead swallow, with its beautiful wings pressed close to its sides and its feet and head drawn under its feathers; the poor bird had certainly died of cold. This grieved Thumbelina very much; she was very fond of all the little birds who had sung and twittered so beautifully to her all the summer. But the mole kicked him with his crooked legs, and said, "He doesn't pipe any more now. How miserable it must be to be born a little bird! Thank Heaven, that can happen to none of my children; such a bird has nothing but his tweet, and is obliged to starve in winter."

"Yes, you may well say that as a sensible man," said the field-mouse. "What does the bird get for all his twittering when winter comes? He must starve and freeze. But I suppose that is considered very grand."

Thumbelina said nothing; but when the two others had turned their backs upon the bird, she bent down, and putting the feathers aside which covered his head, she kissed him upon his closed eyes.

"Perhaps it was he who sang so beautifully to me in the summer," she thought. "How much pleasure he has given me, the dear, beautiful bird!"

The mole now stopped up the hole through which the daylight shone in, and then accompanied the ladies home. But at night Thumbelina could get no sleep; so she got up from her bed and wove a fine large carpet of hay, which she carried along, and spread out over the dead bird. She also laid the tender stamina of flowers, which were as soft as cotton, and which she had found in the field-mouse's room, around the bird, so that he might lie warm.

"Good-bye, you beautiful little bird," she said. "Good-bye and many thanks for your beautiful singing in summer, when all the trees were green and the sun shone down warm upon us." Then she laid her head upon the bird's heart. But the bird was not dead; he was only lying there benumbed, and having now been warmed again was coming back to life.

In autumn all the swallows fly away to warm countries; but if there is one who is belated, it gets so frozen that it drops down as if dead, and remains lying where it falls, and soon the cold snow covers it.

Thumbelina trembled, so frightened was she, for the bird was big, very big, compared with her, who was only an inch long. But she took courage, and laying the cotton more closely round the poor swallow, she fetched a leaf of mint which she herself had used as a blanket, and laid it over the bird's head.

The next night she again stole up to him; he was alive, but very weak, and could open his eyes only for a short moment to look at Thumbelina, who stood before him with a piece of decaying wood in her hand, for she had no other lantern.

"Thank you, my pretty little child," said the sick swallow to her. "I have been so beautifully warm. Soon I shall get my strength back and will then be able to fly about in the warm sunshine outside."

"Oh!" said she, "it is cold outside; it is snowing and freezing. Stay in your warm bed; I will take care of you."

Then she brought the swallow some water in a leaf of a flower. This the swallow drank, and told her how he had torn one of his wings on a thorn-bush, and had therefore been unable to fly so quickly as the other swallows who had flown far away to warm countries. So he had at last fallen to the ground, but could not remember anything more, and did not at all know how he had come there.

So he remained down there the whole winter, and Thumbelina nursed and tended him with all her heart; neither the mole nor the field-mouse knew anything about it, for they did not like the poor swallow at all.

As soon as spring came, and the sun warmed the earth, the swallow said good-bye to Thumbelina, who opened the hole which the mole had made up above. The sun shone in beautifully upon them, and the swallow asked her whether she would go with him; she could sit upon his back, he said, and they would fly far into the green forest. But Thumbelina knew that it would grieve the old field-mouse if she left her like that. "No, I cannot," she said.

"Good-bye, good-bye, you good pretty little girl!" said the swallow, and flew out into the sunshine. Thumbelina looked after him, and the tears came into her eyes, for she was very fond of the poor swallow.

"Tweet, tweet," sang the bird and flew into the green forest. Thumbelina was very sad. She got no permission to go out into the warm sunshine. The corn which had been sown on the field over the house of the field-mouse grew up high into the air; it was a thick wood for the poor little girl who was only an inch high.

"Now you are a bride, Thumbelina," said the field-mouse. "Our neighbor has asked for your hand. What a great piece of luck for a poor child! Now you will have to make your outfit, both woolen and linen clothes; for you must lack nothing when you are the mole's wife."

Thumbelina had to turn the spindle, and the field-mouse hired four spiders to weave for her day and night. Every evening the mole used to visit them, and was always saying that at the end of the summer, the sun would not shine so warm by a long way, that it was burning the earth as hard as a stone. Yes, when the summer was over, he would celebrate his marriage with Thumbelina. But the latter was not at all pleased, for she could not bear the tiresome mole. Every morning when the sun rose, and every evening when it set she stole out to the door, and when the wind parted the ears of corn, so that she could see the blue sky, she would think how bright and beautiful it was out there, and would have a great longing to see the dear swallow again. But he never came back; he had probably flown far away into the beautiful green wood.

When autumn came, Thumbelina had her whole outfit ready.

"You are to be married in four weeks," said the field-mouse to her. But Thumbelina wept, and said she would not have the tiresome mole.

"Fiddlesticks!" said the field-mouse; "don't be obstinate, or I will bite you with my white teeth. He is a fine man whom you are going to marry. The Queen herself has not such black velvety fur. He has a full kitchen and cellar. Be thankful for it!"

Now the wedding was to take place. The mole had already come to fetch Thumbelina; she was to live with him deep down under the earth, and never come out to the warm sunshine, for that he did not like. The poor little girl was very sad; she was now to say good-bye to the beautiful sun, which, while she lived with the field-mouse, she had always had permission to look at from the door. "Good-bye, bright sun!" she said, and stretched her arms out high, and walked a little way off from the house of the field-mouse, for now the corn was cut and there remained only the dry stubbles. "Good-bye, good-bye!" she said, and wound her arms round a little red flower which was still blooming there. "Greet the little swallow for me if you see him."

"Tweet, tweet," suddenly sounded above her head; she looked up, and saw the little swallow, who was just flying by. When he spied Thumbelina, he was very pleased; she told him how unwilling she was to marry the ugly mole, and that she would have to live deep down under the earth, where the sun never shone. She could not help crying in telling it.

"The cold winter is coming now," said the swallow; "I am flying away to warm countries; will you come with me? You can sit on my back; then we shall fly away from the ugly mole and his dark room, far away over the mountains, to warm countries, where the sun shines more beautifully than here, where it is always summer and there are glorious flowers. Do fly with me, dear little Thumbelina — you who saved my life when I lay frozen in the dark underground cellar."

"Yes, I will go with you," said Thumbelina; and she seated herself on the bird's back, with her feet on his outspread wing, binding her girdle fast to one of his strongest feathers. Then the swallow flew up into the air, over forest and sea, high up over the great mountains, where snow always lies. And Thumbelina began to freeze in the cold air, but then she crept under the bird's warm feathers, and only put out her little head to admire all the beauty beneath her.

At last they came to the warm countries. There the sun shone far brighter than here, the sky seemed twice as high, and in the ditches and on the hedges grew the finest green and blue grapes. In the woods hung citron and oranges; the air was heavy with the scent of myrtle and mint, and on the high roads the prettiest little children ran and played with large colored butterflies. But the swallow flew still farther, and it became more and more beautiful. Under the most majestic green trees by the blue lake stood a marble castle of dazzling whiteness, all of the olden time. Vines wound themselves round the tall pillars, and up above there were a number of swallows' nests, and in one of these lived the swallow who was carrying Thumbelina.

"This is my house," said the swallow. "But it would not be proper for you to live with me here, and my arrangements are not such as you would be satisfied with. Pick out for yourself one of the most beautiful flowers that are growing down there; then I will put you into it, and you shall have everything as nice as you can wish."

"That is glorious!" she said, clapping her little hands.

There lay a large white marble pillar which had fallen to the ground and broken into three pieces; between these grew the finest large white flowers. The swallow flew down with Thumbelina, and set her upon one of the broad petals. But what was her surprise! There in the middle of the flower sat a little man, as white and transparent as if he were made of glass; he wore the prettiest golden crown on his head, and had splendid little wings on his shoulders; he himself was no bigger then Thumbelina. He was the angel of the flower. In every flower lived such a little man or woman; but this one was the king of all.

"Heavens! how beautiful he is!" whispered Thumbelina to the swallow. The little prince was very frightened at the sight of the swallow, for it was a giant bird compared to him, who was so small and delicate. But when he spied Thumbelina he was greatly pleased; she was the prettiest little girl he had ever seen. He therefore took his golden crown from off his head, and put it upon hers, asking her what her name was, and whether she would be his wife; then she should be queen of all the flowers. He was indeed quite a

different man to the son of the toad, and the mole with the black velvety fur. She said "Yes" to the grand prince. And out of every flower came a lady and a gentleman, so dainty that they were a pleasure to behold. Each one brought Thumbelina a present; but the best of all was a pair of beautiful wings from a large white fly; these were fastened onto Thumbelina's back, and now she could fly from flower to flower. There was much rejoicing, and the little swallow sat up in his nest, and was to sing the bridal song; this he did as well as he could, although in his heart he was sad, for he was so fond of Thumbelina, and would have liked never to separate himself from her.

"You shall not be called Thumbelina," said the Flower Angel to her. "That is an ugly name and you are too pretty for it. We will call you Maia." "Good-bye, good-bye!" said the little swallow with a heavy heart, and flew away from the warm countries back to Denmark. There he had a little nest over the window where the man lives who can tell tales. To him he sang "Tweet, tweet." That is how we know the whole story.